Magical Potters

By Peter L. Barnes

www.peterlbarnes.com

Published by Blissetts
www.blissetts.com

BLISSETTS
EST? 1920

This book is dedicated to Lyndy, who inspired me to write, after the loss of my daughter Kirsty.

Amazon Kindle print edition

© Peter Barnett

Peter Barnett asserts the moral right to be identified as the author of this book writing under the name of Peter L. Barnes. Front cover by Geng Gendall.

A catalogue record for this book is available from the British Library.

ISBN 9781521936436

A supernatural story of love; heartache; betrayal and revenge.

Chapters

Prologue - Prowling 1201..................................6

Chapter 1 - Cornish Tin Mines, 1795 8

Chapter 2 - Darkest Thoughts...........................12

Chapter 3 - Betrayal in the Mine 15

Chapter 4 - The Miner's Lies.............................22

Chapter 5 - Brianna Accuses............................24

Chapter 6 – Brianna's Visions in the Pool.................27

Chapter 7 - Grabbing Power 31

Chapter 8 - Brianna and the Sprites 40

Chapter 9 – Caught in the Act 44

Chapter 10 – Power Corrupts...........................54

Chapter 11 - Brianna in the Dark 61

Chapter 13 – Trapped Forever 67

Chapter 14 – The China Talks.........................75

Chapter 15 – Sleight of Hand...........................78

Chapter 16 - Manacles in the Dungeon 81

Chapter 17 - Miners Materialise 86

Chapter 18 - Jan Loses It..91

Chapter 19 - Monsters in the Pool 95

Chapter 20 - Lion Dogs Attack 100

Chapter 21 - Haunting Jan 108

22 –Beatrice Deceived 114

Chapter 23 - Crystal Horrified 121

Chapter 24 – Cold Dishes......................................127

Chapter 25 – Visions in a Pool...............................135

Chapter 26 – Two in a Bed 137

Chapter 27 – Locked In...141

Prologue - Prowling 1201

It prowled through the village, stopping only to test the air for human scent. Years had passed since it had last slunk from the caverns, ever terrified of brightness and of the coming dawn, which would send it raving mad. The night's dark clouds shrouded the creature well, providing a sense of security and hope. Driven by primeval instincts and needs, it flitted from shadowy lane to dark doorway, purposely avoiding the glows from the houses' windows.

It stood snorting and snuffling, hidden from the small stone cottages either side of the road, little night bugs scuttling away. Seeking out the scent of the blood of small children, the dark creature stopped in front of one promising looking house. Being slightly larger than the others, maybe there were small children inside, it thought hopefully.

Squinting through fingers to avoid the brightness from within, it peered through the small window. A large group of people snuggled close to the fire and each other in an effort to keep warm. The glow from the small fire was almost too much for its eyes, but it had to see for itself if there were children inside. Three small children sat in front of the fire chatting and giggling, the creature growled excitedly.

Creeping quietly around the back of the house there was more opportunity, a small stream serving as their waste disposal, which smelt delicious to the creature. It did not have to wait long. A small girl emerged from the back of the house in a grey linen dress, nervously looking around, before rushing to the stream.

Not wasting a second, the creature rushed across and grabbed her. Holding one gnarled hand across her mouth to prevent her screams rousing the men folk, it picked her up effortlessly and raced across the cliffs towards the beach. The child was feisty and continued to struggle and despite the creature's strength, she was slowing it down. The squirming child was becoming too much of a nuisance, so it cuffed her around the head to bully her into submission.

At last, arriving at the cave entrance, the creature felt sure it was safe from pursuit. Dragging and forcing the child into the back of the cave and down a narrow passage, clambering deeper and deeper into the depths under the sea. The girl was now so terrified, she never uttered a sound, she whimpered despairingly, her face crinkling up and tears creeping into the corners of her eyes. Desperate to be home in the comfort of her family but she knew somehow that that life was behind her.

The creature finally reached the safety of the cavern and bellowed in an ancient Celtic tongue, "Orthol, I have one!"

A large shadow appeared from the back of the cavern.

"Show me her veins," growled Orthol, in the same guttural language.

The creature held up the small child and waved her about, exposing her arms, blood pumping as her small legs kicked out futilely.

"Excellent, she is wonderful, take her down."

Back in the village the disappearance had caused panic and the cries of "Letitia, Letitia, where are you?" rang across the bleak Cornish hills, but Letitia was never seen again and tears rolled down cheeks.

Chapter 1 - Cornish Tin Mines, 1795

"Hey guys look at this!" Jan shouted. His short pick had broken through into an underground cave at the end of the cramped tunnel. After a long day, down in the black mines, trying to eke out more than the miserable existence, maybe a new cavern might hold some promise. Long days of hard work, hammering, chipping and sweating brought little reward but at least the brothers were working for themselves these days.

Their minds and bodies were used to the stale damp air, the oppressive darkness punctuated by their dim candles stuck to their hardened cloth hats. They spent so long down in the mine starting their daily drudgery before sunrise and finishing after sunset, it meant they hardy saw daylight. The sounds of dripping water echoing off the hard-confined walls the only music they heard, missing most of the daylight birdsong.

"What?" called Mark.

"A new cave," Jan called back.

"Let me see," said Tom, holding his tallow candle forward into the entrance. Their eyes accustomed to the dark mines could just make out the steep drop that opened up in front of them. A myriad of colours twinkled out from the depths, candlelight reflecting off the walls. A strange fishy smell drifted out of the opening and more than the usual watery sounds emanated from the black hole beneath them.

"This is just the chance we need," cried Jan. They had hoped for some luck for years, ever since taking over the workings of the disused mine. Almost completely worked out and depleted of the tin, the brothers had eked out a miserable existence from the scraps of minerals left down here. It was marginally better than working for the tiny wages of the mines up the coast. It had almost killed them a few times through rock falls and unseen hazards, all with little reward.

"Well there is no way we can get in there and out of

it without more ropes," said Tom. "I don't intend to be trapped again." He shuddered at the memory of the night he'd spent in the dark abyss when he'd slipped down a crevice into a void.

"Let's get back to our store and collect what we need, ropes and shoring no doubt," said Jan.

"We're coming back today?" queried Mark.

"Of course, today, let's go. Be careful though," said Tom. "We may be in a rush but we still have to be wary, we don't want to be caught out by the traps we've set up for thieves."

"What do you think is down there?" asked Tom as they made the way back to their stash of supplies near the entrance to the mine.

"Riches beyond our dreams I hope. We know the tin seam goes into the cave but I'm sure I could see more than just tin." Jan replied. "Copper for sure and maybe some gold."

"Fool's Gold more likely. We can only survive so long on turnips and water," said Mark, thinking of his three daughters.

"Don't be such a pessimist Mark. You shouldn't have so many children. This is the breakthrough we deserve, I can feel it in my bones," said Tom.

They collected ropes and wooden planks. "Thankfully the early miners couldn't be bothered to remove all this material, no doubt too much trouble to drag out when it was abandoned," said Jan.

Slowly they crawled on through the tunnels, stooping to avoid overhanging rocks and avoiding all their traps and dead ends. The light from the candles created weird shapes and shadows which never failed to haunt Mark.

"Right let's get digging," said Tom, once they were back at the new cave.

Carefully removing the rocks that hid the new

cavern, they re- opened a small hole to the entrance.

"Strange breeze," whispered Mark as a wisp of air moved through the mine.

"Must be from the cavern," Jan replied, "but fresh air is good, less chance of an explosion."

"Well fresh is not the word I would use, more like stale fish," said Mark.

"Come on, look through. See what you think."

Jan held up a larger candle and peered into the darkness and could now clearly see some flickering colours reflecting off the walls. "By Jove, what's that? We need to get in there."

"Put up some more shoring, that roof still doesn't look too safe." said Jan. "I'm not getting killed by a rock fall now."

They inserting the props and gradually opened the hole sufficiently for them to get through. Jan peered over the drop, in front of them. "Looks safe enough to me, tie the rope up."

"Ok, I'm first, being the eldest," said Tom excitedly. "Leave an extra candle up here so we can find our way out."

Gingerly, Tom climbed down the rope to the floor; Jan and Mark quickly followed into the cool, huge cavern. The sheer size of the cavern meant that the dim light from the candles didn't even show the far sides. Light reflected from glistening stalactites hanging from the roof. Jan realised that their wildest dreams were going to come true. His eyes were accustomed to years of darkness so he could quickly make out some of the riches of the cave. Apart from what looked like a rock face of copper ore on the left, there was a thick seam of black tin oxide and amazingly speckles of gold.

"Look, a gold seam over there!" exclaimed Mark, "we're made for life."

They went over to the wall which was gleaming with

specs of gold "No 'fool's gold' this," announced Jan excitedly. The other wall was covered in a damp green surface of the copper node; he ran his hand lovingly over the wet wall.

"There must be 10 years of copper ore over here," Jan shouted. "Where are we going to start?" They hugged each other, relieved that their struggles over the last few years were finally over.

Just at that moment there was a faint rustling in the distance. "What was that? This place is disturbing; I knew I shouldn't have come down this far." Mark's nerves playing up as usual.

"Just that breeze coming through," soothed Tom, but looking down he saw some small crabs scuttling along the floor; they were obviously attracted by the lights but seemingly frightened of their own shadows. "See! Just crabs."

They looked around to check if there were any other more dangerous creatures around. A distant rumbling sound emanated from the far end of the cavern, slowly building into a crescendo.

"Rock fall!" shouted Mark.

"Nothing like any I've heard," Jan said, now very wary of this place. "Maybe we should just let the place settle down and come back tomorrow with ...."

Sounds, like a team of snorting cart horses charging over cobblestones, filled the cavern and the three miners cowered back as some huge shapes burst through the end of the tunnel and raced towards them. Five monsters bore down on them, hissing, growling and shouting, spitting green slime from their gaping mouths full of sharp long teeth. Resembling upright sharks with hard green tinged, scaly bodies, they balanced on their tails and ran towards the brothers on their short stubby back legs.

Images flashed through Jan's mind, as total fear ran through his blood. Jan threw his short mining pick at one of the charging creatures which buried in its chest but didn't stop the rush. Turning, Jan scrambled for the rope and safety, hearing Tom and Mark screaming as they were caught. Jan almost made it before he was brutally pinned to the wall, the stench of rotten fishy breath enveloping him, just as the huge body was crushing him and threatened to squeeze the air out of his lungs. Jan's final thoughts were of his boys.

Chapter 2 - Darkest Thoughts

The long claws of the monster moved towards his throat and Jan felt them starting to dig into his flesh, piercing the skin. He prayed for intervention but these creatures were obviously not of a mind to give mercy.

"Stop!" roared a voice from the darkness, "let me see them."

The monster lifted Jan up and turned him to face the cavern. In the dimming light of the flickering candles, all Jan could see was a dark mass far back in the cave.

"What are you doing down here?" something roared, in a tongue reminding Jan of ancient Celtic, which Jan understood but he was too frightened to speak.

"Tell me or you die now."

"We're only simple miners, let us go and we'll never return," whimpered Mark, who was now bleeding from several cuts on his body and neck.

"Miners! Come to steal my gold no doubt." The disembodied guttural voice, making his words difficult to understand. "But what use is gold to me without life. Do you have issue?"

"Issue?"

"Offspring, children? Your bodies are not much use to me and I need young sweet blood, preferably female blood."

Terrifying thoughts drifted through Jan's brain. It was well known in these parts that many young children had disappeared across the decades, maybe even longer. Legends of the Roman god Lamia or just Arab slave traders always came to mind.

"I need an answer or the Borgats will slit your throats and leave you to bleed slowly and painfully to death. An agonizing way to go, believe me."

"We all have children, but not for you. We would

rather die," said Tom defiantly. Tom watched as claws slashed across his body and blood sprayed over walls and splattered onto the floor. Tom screamed and tried to fight back but these monsters were just so overpowering.

"Stake him to the wall." The fourth creature brought a sharpened iron stake and holding it to Tom's hand, hammered through it into the rock with a mighty blow from his fist, then did the same with his other hand. Tom fainted away from the pain and loss of blood.

"And what about you?" growled the voice.

"Never," cried Mark. His defiance was also short lived and he was similarly brutally pinned to the wall. Jan trembled, trying to think of a way to get out of here but helpless in the grip of his captor.

"What do I get out of it, if I bring you a child?" Jan said, desperate to escape.

"Your freedom of course and maybe that of your friends. Then if you are lucky, you will get some trinkets! However, be careful what you wish for, as this is not a simple task. The first child has to be your bloodline and at least one from every generation. "

"Trinkets mean nothing," Jan said, ignoring the additional threat. "I need more than that for a child." He knew that he had to find a way out of here first, the thought of stakes being driven through his hands and being left to die slowly as his blood drained from his body, making him desperate. The blood pouring from his brothers' hands and cuts were horrifying and if he could find any way out of here he would take it. "And I need them to be freed as well."

"Trinkets to me will mean a lifetime of luxury for you," answered the monster in the dark. "Every child you bring me will get a reward. However, I shall keep your brothers as hostages until you return. Do we have a deal? Of course, should you not return, I will send the Borgats after you and hunt you and your families to extinction!"

Jan knew that he had to get out of their clutches, only then could he plan what to do. But he could do nothing unless he accepted the demands, however improbable. "Agreed!" All Jan could think of was the imagined riches rather than the plight of his brothers.

"You have until dawn tomorrow to return with the girl child. Let him go."

The Borgat reluctantly released Jan and he immediately scrambled for the rope and raced out of the cavern as fast as he could and up into the tunnels. He hoped that the opening was too small for the monsters and decided not to wait around to find out. Jan couldn't believe his luck at not only escaping the monsters but also the chance of obtaining the promised riches.

His mind raced almost as fast as his pulse. Jan had two boys so there was no way he could give the monster a female of his own blood line. How was he going to solve this? He reached the bottom of the final ladder at the same time as the depths of his soul, when a thought struck him. He would bring one of Mark's girls as the sacrifice, surely it was still bloodline. This would keep his own children safe, as well as providing a good life for them. He doubted whether his brothers would survive the ordeal below, so he wrote them off anyway, leaving him to concentrate on his own needs.

He finally emerged at the mine entrance thankful for his escape from the horrors beneath. He had no idea what wrath the monsters could effect from their dungeons if any but the promise of untold riches had changed him forever. Now the question was how was he going to snatch one of the girls, without being seen or suspected? Despite being midday, the dark clouds and misty rain made visibility almost non-existent. Maybe he still had a chance of pulling this off.

Chapter 3 - Betrayal in the Mine

Jan trundled home full of dark thoughts and grateful that he had, for the time being, escaped the clutches of the monsters. The thought of the riches that the monster had promised him made him determined to find a way to appease them and claim his reward.

As Jan approached the group of houses where he and his brothers' families lived, he realised chance had provided him with the perfect opportunity. He spied little Clarissa playing mud pies out in the back gardens.

"Clarissa, Clarissa," he called quietly to the little girl. "Come here quickly, your Daddy is looking for you"

"What? Oh Unky, look, see my lully pies," Clarissa cried out in her baby voice. "Do you want some?" Holding out the muddy lumps to him, in her tiny hands, she looked up at him with innocent blue eyes that almost made him change his mind but his course was set. He swallowed hard and concentrated on his future life of luxury.

"Tell you what, let's take one for your Daddy's lunch." Jan whisked her up in his arms, the mud pie still in her hand. "He'll be so happy to see you."

Trusting her uncle as she always had, Clarissa clung on to him as he rushed back over the hills, hoping no-one had seen them.

"Where Daddy, unky Jan?"

"He's at the mine, sweetheart. He can't wait to see you and get his lunch."

"Goodie."

Jan hurried back to the mine entrance. "I'll have to carry you down the ladder and then you can run and see him." Jan steeled himself for the next meeting, hoping that the monster's need for young blood was going to be satisfied.

"Dark, unky Jan. Where Daddy?"

"Only a few more steps. Let me hold the light up, that will make it easier for you," Jan said, lighting a second candle so that some of the shadows receded. They walked along the tunnel for a long time, Clarissa clutching Jan's hand very tightly, until they were close to the opening.

"Scared, unky."

Jan squeezed her hand reassuringly. "Not long now, darling. Now your Dad is down the hole and I am going to lower you on the rope. Don't forget his pie."

Clarissa still clutched the remnants of the pies in her tiny hands. "Daddy, pie!" she called.

Jan tied the rope around her waist and got ready to lower her down. To his horror, Jan could hear groans coming from the cavern which he knew were from his brothers and in the distance, he could hear the heavy snorting from the creatures that called themselves Borgats.

"Dark, don't like it, help, Daddy!" Clarissa screamed.

"Run, Clarissa, run!" called Mark.

"Daddy, Daddy!"

Jan became desperate as he could see his plan going awry. Forcing a calmness into his voice that he didn't feel, he picked up Clarissa and held onto her tightly. "See? I told you your Daddy was waiting for you."

She was struggling to get free now but it was too late as Jan lowered her to the floor. The lamps down there were almost out but Jan could still make out his brothers pinned against the wall. Jan let go of the rope and Clarissa ran as fast as she could and wrapped her arms around her father.

"Help me, help me, Daddy, scared. I got your lunch."

"Stay calm, Clarissa. I'm sure your Uncle will take

you home now, won't you, Jan?" pleaded Mark, his voice now weak and barely audible.

A disembodied voice boomed from the back of the cavern, "Oh how delicious. A betrayal by a brother, you really are a despicable man. I love it! Her blood will taste all the sweeter!"

Clarissa continued to sob, clinging to her father's legs.

"You monster!" shouted Tom at his brother.

"Don't kill her," called Mark.

"Kill!" drooled the monster, "oh no but I shall be borrowing her blood, the more the merrier."

"Leaving us for your own safety, I can understand Jan, but giving Clarissa away is unforgivable," said Tom. He screamed as one of the Borgats slashed his claws across Tom's chest, opening up new wounds.

"Where are my jewels?" Jan shouted, ignoring the pleas of his brother.

"Give him the jewels and gold," ordered the monster, from the cover of the dark. One of the Borgats threw a pouch through the opening. Jan quickly picked it up and even in the dim light could see huge jewels, gold coins and nuggets glinting from within as he held his candle to look inside. A wicked grin spread across his face, there was fortune here, more than anything he had seen. Jan was relieved he didn't have to climb down in to the cavern, since he was sure that having delivered the sacrifice he would not have been allowed to leave.

The monster spoke and his tone was menacing. "Don't forget, each time you deliver a child there will be more rewards for you. But I specifically expect a fresh child from the family line, every generation, preferably a girl, as they are so much sweeter."

Jan began to replace rocks around the entrance, blanking out the cries of his niece and pleas from Tom.

"Don't think that blocking the exit will save you

from retribution as there are many ways out of here, so if you don't return we will definitely come up and find you," continued the voice from the dark.

Jan paused from his task, his mind consumed with greed. He shouted back to the monster.

"There is not enough reward here. She is flesh and blood after all."

"Not yours though, you greedy bastard," shouted Tom, through gritted teeth.

"Give him a little more," called the monster. "Now leave us."

The Borgats threw a second bag of trinkets. Jan grinned, pocketing the second bag.

"Jan, as God is our witness, we will haunt you and your heirs for ever!" yelled Tom, but Jan was too busy collecting his trophies to hear or care.

He backed up the cave and proceeded to disguise the hole where they had broken through, making it look like a rock fall should anyone come down here again, which he doubted after the tales he would tell.

As the final gap was filled he could still hear the faint screams of Clarissa and the accusations of his brothers. He decided he would come back later and make some more complex traps, but meanwhile he had to get back and cover his tracks.

He carefully stashed away the large pouch of jewels in a hidden alcove. He kept a portion of the gold nuggets and a couple of stones with which he hoped were diamonds and rubies. His conscience and morality was suppressed now by his joy in his newly ill begotten wealth. He would take his family well away from here and start a new life.

He examined his clothes and body to make sure he looked as though he had crawled out of a rock fall. He roughed up his already filthy work clothes and spread some blood from his wounds across his chest. He added some cuts to himself with his pocket knife and scraped his fingers across some sharp rocks. He felt he could now go back to his village and play out the second part of his plan. Jan slowly trudged back to his cottage, making up a plausible story as he went.

Building up courage and assuming a grief-stricken voice, he burst into his cottage.

"Disaster, disaster," he shouted to his wife, feigning a horror he no longer felt. "The entire mine collapsed, my brothers are crushed."

"Oh no, a mine collapse as well!" said Maeve.

"As well?" queried Jan, feigning ignorance.

"It's Clarissa, she's gone missing, we had no idea there was also a problem down the mine," cried Maeve. "Is there no hope for your brothers?"

"None I'm afraid," said Jan, hanging his head. "Now, what's this about Clarissa?"

"No-one has seen her for hours," said Maeve. "They set up a search party. If you're up to it, we need to help."

"I've lost my brothers, but yes we can't grieve yet," said Jan. "We have to find Clarissa, I'm sure she's wandered off somewhere. It would be a double tragedy for the family if we can't find her."

"How are we going to break the news to the wives, they're already distraught," said Maeve.

"There's no easy way. Back to Clarissa, did anybody upset her?"

"Of course not! She was outside playing in the mud and nobody saw her disappear."

Thank god for that, thought Jan. "There, there Maeve, I'm sure Clarissa's close by, she certainly wasn't near the mines, I would have seen her on my way back. Anyway, we'll have to go and give June and Marion the sad news about their husbands." Jan gave her another hug. "Let's go."

Jan gathered himself up for more displays of grief and accompanied Maeve next door to see the other families.

Tom's and Mark's wives, already distraught over Clarissa, burst out crying when Jan explained the double tragedy.

"Tom and Mark, dead! What will become of us now?" cried Tom's wife, June. She flung her arms around Marion and together they held each other as they wept for their fallen husbands.

"But what's this about Clarissa? Have we got search parties out?" said Jan, still searching for a distraction.

John, one of their neighbours and a village elder, was also with the wives. "We've come back from our search to get lanterns and sustenance. We're off now Jan, are you able to join us?"

"Yes of course, she's my niece you know. If we can find her that would certainly be one blessing for the day. I'm sure I can do something to help." He followed John out of the door knowing that there was no way they would find her.

It was nearly dawn when a very wet and tired and seemingly dispirited Jan returned. Maeve was still looking after the other wives.

They looked up. "Any sign of her?" a look of desperation in their eyes.

"None, I'm afraid. We'll search again later in the morning. I'm still sure she has only wandered off. It's very difficult to search everywhere in the dark, there are so many places to hide."

"But she's so tiny she couldn't have gone far," said Maeve.

"Sadly, there are so many holes, caves and wells. She could have easily fallen in and we would never find her," said Jan.

"We must all get some rest otherwise we will be too worn out for a thorough search in the morning and may miss some vital clues," said Maeve. "Come on Jan you look exhausted."

Once home Maeve stoked up the fire, boiled a kettle of water and started helping Jan to clean up and wash the cuts and grazes on his hands and chest.

The next morning, much to Jan's delight, it was pouring with rain. Hopefully this would cover any tracks he and Clarissa had made. He also helped direct the search towards the local town to throw the party off the scent, talking about gypsies and vagabonds that the towns harboured. It was four days before the search was called off.

Jan sat with his family as they held a memorial service for his brothers and said prayers for the safe return of Clarissa in the local chapel. He squirmed uncomfortably when the preacher praised Jan for his efforts to save his brothers and tireless efforts to find the child.

The sun shone through the coloured images in the window behind the preacher. The preacher droned on, glad to have a full congregation for a change. Jan's attention drifted away from the words and to the hazy images behind his head. Gradually the images changed to the faces of his dead brothers, maggots crawling through their eye sockets, hands replaced by the claws of the Borgats, sharp teeth dripping with blood and body parts. Jan leapt up screaming and raced down the aisle of the chapel and out through the churchyard, pursued by the monstrous creations of his mind.

Chapter 4 - The Miner's Lies

Jan avoided the church after his scare, even though he decided the apparition was an over anxious reaction to the events and his fear of discovery. Nevertheless, he decided a move away from the area would be for the best. However, before doing so, he needed to clear up the affairs regarding June and Marion, his brothers' widows. Composing himself, he went around to their tiny home.

"Any news?" asked Marion hopefully.

"On Clarissa, nothing I'm afraid but I'm sure she will turn up soon," said Jan.

June collapsed back again into Marion's arms. "And no hope for our husbands."

"None I'm afraid."

"What's to become of us?" sobbed June.

"I am so very sorry that I couldn't save your husbands," he told them. "The mine's much too unstable to go back to recover their bodies, I'm afraid."

"I'm sure you did everything you could," said Marion. "You and your brothers were close. How are you coping?"

"Not good, my underground days are definitely over," said Jan.

"What are we going to do, there's no money - we'll starve," cried June.

Jan had to make the most of the opportunity to fulfil his dark obligations. He knew he had to guarantee the female line, so it was time to put his plans into place.

"We've had a collection around the village and the neighbours put together a small sum to help you both out. I managed to force the smelter owner into paying the money that he owed." Lies rolled off his tongue almost as easily as the tears rolled down their faces.

"That's very kind," said Marion, "but what about the future?"

"I've shared a fair portion of what was owed. As you remember we had all bequeathed the proceeds from the mine to each other in the event of any mishap," continued Jan. "Should there be anything I can do in future, I will help where I can."

"Anything to help the girls would be wonderful," said Marion, who was coping much better than June.

Certainly will, he thought, but out loud said, "I can't promise much of course, it'll depend on what work I can get."

Marion looked up. "Of course, you also have to look after your own family first."

"True enough," Jan said. "But it is the least I can do for my brothers." He had no intention of getting rid of his golden goose, but they weren't to know that.

"Thank you, Jan, I know it can't be easy for you either," said Marion.

"So how are the other children coping?" Jan enquired. Marion had three girls aged from eight to twelve and June had one other daughter and a son.

Before she could reply there was a commotion at the door as June's eldest daughter Brianna came bursting through to the kitchen. Hands on her small hips, she stood her ground facing Jan. Staring into his face she yelled, "You. It was you!"

"What are you talking about?" said Marion. "Don't be so rude to Uncle Jan, he's trying to help us."

"I saw you! I saw you!"

"I don't understand what you are talking about," said Jan, fearful now that he might have been seen.

"I saw you taking Clarissa!"

Chapter 5 - Brianna Accuses

"You were there in my dream, taking Clarissa," she screamed.

"Dreams, what dreams?" asked June.

"I dreamt Uncle Jan took Clarissa," she continued, her tears forming little white lines down her grubby cheeks.

"I'm sorry Brianna you can't accuse someone because you had a dream," said Marion. "Your Uncle has been very kind."

"I don't know what you are talking about, Brianna. I was down in the mine trying to rescue your father when she was taken." That was a relief thought Jan, for a minute he thought he really had been seen. After the vision in the chapel the last thing he needed were the accusations from his family.

"Brianna, please apologise to Uncle Jan and then go to bed," snapped June, embarrassed by the tirade.

"Never! I know, I just know!" Brianna ran from the kitchen sobbing.

"I'm terribly sorry Jan, she's never acted like that before," said Marion. "I wonder where she gets these ideas."

"I am sure she is upset over all the events and hopefully, in time, she'll get over it," said Jan. "I will be taking over the mine as per our agreement but there is a small payment due to you both. I'll have the documents drawn up and then I can give you the money. I'll see you in a couple of days to get your marks."

Jan left the house and had the feeling that Brianna was watching him. How could Brianna possibly know? The Borgats may get a bonus if she didn't shut up, he thought. He was glad that most of the work of sealing the mine entrance was complete; he certainly didn't want her poking around. Maybe he would have to set even more traps.

He walked away slowly from the cottage, feeling Brianna's eyes boring into the back of his head. Determined to ride this out he trudged away resisting the urge to turn around, sure that Brianna would see straight through his guilt. Fortunately, no-one had believed her vision but he would have to keep a close eye on her.

****

The next day Jan had a thought that Brianna might decide to do some searching of her own. He was not then surprised to see her furtively leave the house and walk slowly towards the cliffs, no doubt searching the ground for any signs of Clarissa. However, after the rain and the footsteps of the searchers in the mud between the rocky outcrops, it would be unlikely that she would find anything, certainly no visible signs. Keeping a low profile, Jan saw her hesitate when she got close to the cliff. She bent over and, squinting, Jan realised what she had seen.

"Damn," he said under his breath. A glint of red between some of the rocks had caught her attention. Reaching down she moved the rocks until she was able to free what must be Clarissa's hair ribbon.

How had he missed that? This was going to prove very difficult. No way could he engineer another disappearance especially after her accusation yesterday. He would have to do some quick thinking to stop another challenge and another disappearance would be too suspicious.

Brianna looked for over an hour in all the small caves and behind all the big rocks. Thankfully for Jan she found nothing else, but the ribbon would have been enough to confirm her suspicions.

Finally, she reached the mine head; Jan couldn't believe she would go down there without a light of some sort. But after a look into the dark gloom, Brianna obviously decided that it would be too dangerous down there and turned away and started trudging home. Jan turned and raced across the moors to beat her to the small village. No-one was in his house thankfully and searching through his wife's clothes until he found a red ribbon similar to Clarissa's.

Entering Marion's home, he triumphantly waved the ribbon. "Look what I found. Isn't this Clarissa's? I found it when I was near the village. I've organised a search over there. Can't stop - I must join them."

"Jan, that's hopeful, isn't it?" said Marion jumping up and giving him a hug.

"Yes, well don't get too excited, it may be another false lead. I must be off and join the search."

He ran out and put his wife's ribbon back before she missed it. He hoped his quick action would make a mockery of Brianna, if she came home also brandishing a ribbon. He raced off towards the village to set up another fruitless search, in case Marion queried his story. He would have to finish the work of closing up the mine tomorrow.

Early next morning Jan set off with his tools and made the new door and then disguised it with a rock wall in front. Not good enough for an adult but it would certainly fool a ten-year-old girl. He then went back to see Marion and June.

"Did you find any signs of Clarissa?" asked Marion.

Jan looked as crestfallen as he could. "Sorry it's another dead end. Nothing we could find anyway, no doubt long gone."

Marion sighed, her last hope gone.

No mention of Brianna's find, thought Jan, hopefully she had kept her mouth shut about what she had found.

"I think you should keep the girls away from the mine, it's extremely dangerous and we don't want any more accidents, do we. I think in view of the disappearance of Clarissa it would be a good idea to make sure none of the children went out on their own."

"Don't worry, we'll keep the girls close from now on," Marion agreed.

Jan, satisfied that his tracks were covered, went back to his family and told them of his plans to move away from the coast, happy that he had, for the time being at least, outmanoeuvred Brianna.

Chapter 6 – Brianna's Visions in the Pool

Brianna woke from a restless sleep, her hair damp from tears shed overnight, both for her sister and father.

"Now don't stray too far from the house today Brianna," said her Mum.

"It didn't help Clarissa did it," she replied.

"Be quiet and no more accusations," continued June. "Do as you're told."

"Yes Mum," said Brianna, having no intention of stopping her search for Clarissa.

"Now I'm off with Marion today to see if I can get some work so I don't need any nonsense from you."

Brianna thought her Mum was being hard on her, she was only trying to help. Brianna knew she would have to be careful of Jan though. She realised that he must have seen her with the ribbon, which is why he had come up with his own story. Tears formed once again as she realised that she would not find her sister easily, nor be able to convince her mum of his dirty deeds.

Watching Jan leaving the previous day, from the tiny window, she had been certain that what she had dreamt was true. She hadn't realised before who it was that she had seen in her dream taking Clarissa away. But when she saw Jan sitting there in the kitchen, it came to her in a flash. She had had many dreams like this in the past, although this was the most real. She wished that she had not blurted out the accusation because now he was aware of her distrust.

After her mother left, she spent the day collecting some firewood in case her Mum needed to warm up after a long day, hoping to get back into her favour. She kept away from the cliffs and a wary eye open for Jan. Deciding to make a small model of her sister, she picked up some clay from the garden. Satisfied with her results, she set it by the fire she had made to warm the house.

"Hello Brianna, oooh nice warm house," said her Mum when she returned, also seeing the new pile of firewood.

"Did you get some work Mum?"

"Yes, but only in the kitchen Brianna," said her mum. "Sorry I was cross with you this morning but you are very precious to me and I don't want to lose you as well."

"That's alright."

"Here, give me a hug," she said holding out her arms.

Brianna enjoyed the warmth of her Mum's arms and the relief of her words.

"Now what's this?" asked her mum, spying the clay doll by the fire.

"Oh, it's Clarissa but careful she very soft."

"Not any more, she's dried by the fire," said her Mum, picking up the model. "She's very beautiful and exactly like her. Did you do it all yourself?"

"Yes," said Brianna worried that her Mum wouldn't approve.

"Shall we make some clothes for her?"

"Oh yes please."

They spent the next few evenings making clothes out of tiny rags, until, in Brianna's eyes, Clarissa came to life in the flickering candlelight.

Brianna kept the Clarissa doll in a small pocket tied to her waist, so they could be together wherever she went. Now that her Mum was away most days she managed to occasionally to avoid the family group, to sneak away to continue to search. Taking a small candle with her to try and search the tunnels, she set off with high hopes to the mine head.

"Oh no, what's he done?" she said to her doll,

holding it up. "Look."

Jan had obviously beaten her to it, the mine head had been altered and the old entrance had been closed off. There was no way Brianna would be able to dig her way into the mines.

"Oh Clarissa, I'm sorry but I can't help you," she wailed at the blocked entrance. "I know you are down there somewhere."

She sadly trudged back over the cliffs full of thoughts on how she could expose Jan and get help to rescue Clarissa, when she spied some meadow flowers and late flowering bulbs growing by a small stream. Maybe she could contact Clarissa through the petals. She had done this before when trying to tell the future through flowers floating in a pool of water. She had imagined that the glints and shadows under the surface had helped her tell the future. There had been no insights of the disasters of recent weeks and nothing came to her today.

Taking her petals, she returned to the mine entrance. There was a small pool of water by the mine and she sat down, taking out the figurine and placing it by her side. She carefully placed the petals on the surface. A glint of yellow caught her eye, some early flowering gorse. She picked a small bunch.

"Ow!" She dropped the gorse into the pond after pricking her finger on the sharp thorns. A drop of blood from her finger splashed into the pool, dispersing amidst the clear water. Immediately a shaft of sunlight shone through the clouds and sparkled off the water. Brianna thought she saw dancing sprites under the flowers but assumed it was the sun glinting on the oil paint. There it was again, the petals started to form words.

Brianna was very interested in words and had taught herself how to read and write. She used to read Bible stories to Clarissa during long summer evenings and had even shown her how to recognise letters. She stared, mesmerised, into the pool and read the words that formed on the surface.

'Please keep me alive B.'

Clarissa always called her B, not being able to handle Brianna. The petals were floating and interchanging rapidly with each other, their colours mingling again to form more words.

'Believe in me and my spirit will live on.'

These words were more than Clarissa knew, how strange, Brianna thought.

'Every time you paint a sprite it will help me live.'

"I promise," Brianna whispered back to the pool.

'More blood will make the promise true for you and your children.'

The tiny droplet of blood from the gorse had been the final touch to open up the communication; now it seemed that more was needed. Brianna was not afraid of a bit of blood, so she jabbed her finger with a gorse spike and drops of blood dripped into the pool. She stirred the pool around mingling the petals and blood.

'I love you B and I will always be in your heart if you remain faithful to your promise' spelt a message in the petals.

"Will I ever be able to rescue you?" Brianna's tears were falling into the pool, making little clear circles in the blood.

But the shaft of sunshine died when the clouds closed over. Brianna cried again and vowed never to lose her faith in Clarissa and determined that one day she would rescue her from her fate.

Chapter 7 - Grabbing Power

Jan went down the mine to collect the second bag of gems to fund the journey and his future. He put in place some complex traps, creating a maze to confuse any future intruders and hopefully forcing them into dead ends and towards chasms.

When he got home he found Maeve with a gold nugget in her hands.

"What's this?" she asked. "Well, I know what it is, what does it mean?"

Damn, thought Jan, it must have dropped out of his bag. "It's the future for us and the boys."

"Where did it come from then?"

"I found it after the mine collapsed," said Jan. "There were two nuggets and I have used the other to give money to Marion and June.

"Is there any more?" she asked hopefully.

"No. That's what I've been searching for over the last few days. If there are any, they're behind the rock fall which is too dangerous to explore."

"What are we going to do now?" asked Maeve.

"It's not enough to live on but enough to give us a new life away from here," said Jan, thankful that she had accepted his version. "I intend to move us all to north Cornwall and I'll get a job at the smelter or the foundry."

He didn't need a job but he needed to explain why he had money in his pocket. Satisfied that he had done all he could to protect the mine and ensure the survival of his nieces, he had bought a horse and trap to carry the family and their simple belongings for the journey north.

Jan and Maeve finally arrived at an inn at the small village of St Erth that had been built up around the ore refinery in north Cornwall.

"I'm going to clean up Maeve. Lay out my Sunday best,"

"Why are you dressing up, Jan?"

"Well I need a job for a start and a place to live, I don't want to look like a broke miner, do I?"

Jan cleaned himself up as best he could, before venturing out. "Maeve, you stay here and look after the boys, I'll be a few hours. I'll organise some food for you with the innkeeper."

"I still don't see why we have to be near the mines," said Maeve. "I thought we had enough to give all that up."

"Don't worry, I'm not going down those blasted tunnels again, I intend to get into the Smelter works if I can."

Jan had a quick word with the inn keeper before venturing out. "Do you know a small house for sale around here?" Jan didn't want to show his new-found wealth too quickly.

"There's a nice house on the hill," said the keeper.

"Price?"

"Could be a bargain, the Jones family have fallen on hard times since the husband died. Let me draw you a map."

"Thanks, Keep. Can you organise a hot meal for the family whilst I'm away?"

"Meat and potatoes do?"

"That's fine and thanks for the information."

Jan felt that things were falling nicely into place; hopefully his luck had turned. The Jones' home was on the edge of the village; he walked through the market place, ignoring the tempting baking smells and sounds of the traders calling to attract customers. Reaching the property on the hill, with views of the smoking smelters to the north and the sea in the distance, Jan looked around the outside of the property. The slightly isolated location would be ideal thought Jan, sufficiently out of the way from any prying eyes.

The house looked in good repair with whitewashed stone walls and a solid wooden door, complete with a garden at the back where a rooster strutted and a few chickens pecked at the ground. He knocked on the door calling, "Mrs Jones?"

The door opened revealing a young woman with two pretty girls with golden curly hair about three years old, hanging onto her skirts. Interesting, thought Jan, these girls could come in useful. Although the monster craved bloodline, it had said it wasn't averse to a bit of variety. God, is he going to be haunted by the needs of the monsters for the rest of his life? Probably, but this was all about self-preservation.

"Hello, who are you?"

"Jan, I understand your house is for sale."

"Sadly yes, my husband was killed in the smelter plant and we need to sell quickly, please come in."

He followed her into first room, comfortable furniture around a stone fireplace. A baby was crying in the back room. "Sorry I'll go and quieten her down."

Jan looked around, ten times better than the hovel he had left.

She returned with a baby in her arms "Let me show you the other rooms."

They went into the kitchen which had a large black stove, plus a table and chairs. In the corner was a cot with another baby sleeping blissfully. "Are they also twins? You must be very proud," thinking a bit of flattery might help his cause.

"My joy and my burden. How am I ever going to cope with them all?"

She showed Jan the two bedrooms, "What do you think?"

"It looks fine to me. What happened to your husband?" he asked, hoping she would be able to give him an insight into the smelting company.

"He was a foreman in the smelter works and I have been told that there was an accident involving faulty equipment."

"Sorry, it must have been a great shock. Is the owner giving you any compensation?"

"Nothing, the owner Mr Treagrove refuses to talk to me."

"Typical. Meanwhile the house will suit us I'm sure," said Jan. After a bit of haggling Jan managed to beat her down to well below market value.

"I don't think that's enough; I need to find somewhere else to live."

Jan's mind was racing "I know of a small property in the south, maybe as part of the deal you could take that." Two sets of twins in the area of the mine would create many possibilities.

They agreed to meet the next day at the Solicitor to finalise contracts and transfer the money.

Jan left, very satisfied with his purchase. Now to tackle Mr Treagrove, the smelter owner, and with his new knowledge, maybe a bit of subterfuge. Armed with information and the germ of a plan and dressed appropriately in older gear, he set off for the local hostelry near the plant, to see if he could talk to some workers from the smelter.

He entered the main room to find a dozen or so workers who were spending their weekly wages on drink and tobacco, a thick fug of cheap tobacco, spilt beer and usual sweaty bodies assailing Jan's nostrils. Deciding the best way to loosen tongues was to buy drinks for everyone, he ordered beers all round. He could well afford a few pints of ale and the huge shout of approval immediately bought him some new friends.

Jan got into conversation with a couple of the workers.

"Jan," holding out his hand.

"Greg and this is Tomas"

After a couple more drinks Jan asked, "so you guys work at the smelter?"

"Treagrove's? Yeah, better than down the mines, feel sorry for the miners all those rock falls, at least we are above ground," said Greg.

"But you must have accidents?"

"Oh yes, but not dangerous ones," said Tomas.

"I heard that someone died here recently, wasn't that an accident?" asked Jan.

"No that was no accident, Jones had a fight with the owner and ended up in the furnace," said Greg.

"Didn't the owner get charged with any crime?"

"Who would give witness? We all need our jobs, no point in sticking our heads in a noose."

"Greg, you've had too much, telling tales like that," chided Tomas.

Finally, Jan had his lever to get into Treagrove's smelter business. Preferring to meet the man at his home, he waited till Sunday for his confrontation. It wasn't difficult to find where he lived and he walked to the nearby mansion to confront Mr Treagrove.

Knocking on the door, Jan already had a story ready to get past the butler.

"Yes?"

"I've come to ask Mr Treagrove about Mr Jones' accident."

"And your name is?"

"Jan, on behalf of Mrs Jones."

"Wait here sir, I'll ask if he can see you," he said, showing Jan into a study.

Mr Treagrove flung open the door. "Who the hell are you and what do you want?"

Jan had faced down many men in his time and this one didn't frighten him. Fat and bloated, he would have no chance against Jan.

"I have a proposition for you Mr Treagrove, I think you'd better listen."

"I don't have to listen to you, now get out."

"I'm sure you don't, however if you don't want the murder of Mr Jones to be investigated, then you probably will."

"Murder! It was an accident."

"Actually, witness statements say the opposite, now sit down and listen before you have a heart attack."

Not used to such insubordination but faced down by the determined Jan, he had no choice.

"Now I can make this all go away in exchange for a small consideration."

"Blackmail, I won't stand for that," said Treagrove, standing up again.

"Sit down! No not blackmail at all but a favour. I need a job as a foreman, I understand that you have that vacancy; second I wish to buy some shares in your business and in exchange I shall buy off Mrs Jones and quash the investigation."

"And why would I do all that for a stranger who bursts into my house?"

Jan was prepared for this and took out two

apparent witness statements, actual two billboards he had ripped down on the way here. He waved them around, then carefully tucked them away. "As I said, because I have these statements. I assure you that it will definitely be to your benefit, I think murderers are still hanged in Cornwall."

"That's outrageous."

"So is murder, now what's it to be? I don't have much time."

"How much do you want to invest?" said Mr Treagrove.

Jan assumed that Mr Treagrove would hope to dupe him out of his investment.

"A considerable amount," said Jan, naming what he thought would excite this greedy man. "Working as the foreman will ensure that my investment is protected."

"Come and see me on Tuesday at the plant and I'll think about it over the weekend, now get out of here."

Jan left, working out all the things he would have to put in place before the meeting.

The next morning, Jan sat in front of a Mr Radcliffe, a local Solicitor.

"I need your services for the next year or two, I'm sure you will find it very lucrative."

"That could be quite expensive,"

Jan realised that many people had tried to get his services for free, unless they were the gentry who probably didn't pay well either.

"I understand your concerns," said Jan. "Will this be sufficient?" Presenting the solicitor with a wad of £5 notes he had obtained from the local bank.

The solicitor looked at the money, "Nothing illegal, I hope," obviously wary. "It's unusual to see so much cash."

"I sold a small mine and now want to move on up the chain," lied Jan. "I'm thinking of buying into the smelter business."

"Very difficult. Bit of a closed shop, that," said Mr Radcliffe.

"I think you'll find that Mr Treagrove will be very amenable to such an investment."

"He's a very tricky customer, I would be surprised if he allowed that."

"He has already agreed in principle, I expect he will try and cheat me so that's where I need your help. I can't read and therefore will have to trust you implicitly. I have also agreed to purchase Mrs Jones house, she should be here shortly to sign an agreement."

"You have been busy."

"I also need you to find me a tutor to help me read and write so that I don't get duped in the future."

"I'm sure that can be arranged. There is an old lady, Jenna, who lives in the woods but originally worked for the local gentry."

There was a knock on the door. "A Mrs Jones is here for you sir."

"Thank you, please show her in."

＊＊＊＊＊＊

Jan arrived at Jenna's little hut in the woods, smoke curled from the open fire drifting into the trees above.

Jenna appeared from the doorway, wrapped in an assortment of colourful robes; smelling of wood smoke, unlit pie hanging from her dry lips. Wrinkles and old pox marks disfigured what would once have been a startling beauty.

"Who are you, get off my land," crackled the old maid.

"Mr Radcliff sent me. He tells me you can help me," said Jan, doubtful that he would get what he wanted from the old women.

"What, that good for nothing son of mine."

"He tells me you can read and write," he said.

"What, you want me to write a love letter? That'll be a shilling," she said, holding out a hand, darkened by earth and charcoal.

"No, I need you to teach me, I'll pay you well," he said holding out a golden sovereign.

The old woman made a grab for the coin but Jan was too quick and snatched it away. Instead he gave her some coins.

"You'll get the rest of your money when you've done your job," he said.

The relationship proved more fruitful for them both as Jenna's skills included a study of herbs and remedy's which Jan absorbed with relish. Paying her on a regular basis meant she opened up more and more. One day when Jan arrived early he found her book of recipes which included some of the more useful poisons, including the properties of digitalis.

Chapter 8 - Brianna and the Sprites

Over the years, Brianna went to the mine head whenever she could get away without being discovered. Fortunately, the locals now considered the place dangerous and even haunted, so once she got there she could try and summon Clarissa without fear of discovery.

She went back to her pool and dropped some dried petals into the water. She stirred the water causing the sun to sparkle off the ripples; then the petals began to settle in patterns. Brianna pricked her finger for the final ingredient, the resulting drop of blood splashed into the water.

"Clarissa, can you hear me? Clarissa, please talk to me. I want to see how I can help."

As the drop of blood spread into the pool a message slowly formed on the surface.

'B free us please'

"I've tried and failed Clarissa."

The petals moved around the pool and formed words once again.

'Make us a magic ring in the woods'

"Why not here?"

'Bad spirits here.'

"Where do you want to put it?"

'In the woods, where we can dance and play.'

"Will that free you?"

'Yes'

"And who is us?" asked Brianna.

Words raced across the pool. 'I am not the first and will not be the last. You cannot free our bodies but you can free our spirits.'

"So how do I make a magic ring?"

'A stone circle around the pool in the wild woods is all we need.'

The petals sunk to the bottom of the pool and a cloud crossed in front of the sun, leaving the pool gloomy and lifeless.

Brianna left the cliffs and walked to a wooded area closer to home. The sun broke through the cloud cover once again and lit up a glade in the woods; a small stream burbled amongst the lush grass. Brianna revelled at the sprinkling of blue and white flowers swaying in the light breeze; her nose filled with the fresh earthy smells of spring, as plants woke to the joys of a new year. Catkins intent on pollination shook free and drifted across the clearing. Brianna listened to the trill of tiny birds setting out their territorial rights, trying to attract mates and deter rivals.

Brianna was going to need some help as the stones in the area were too big and heavy to move and mount on her own. Then she remembered there was a local boy, Paul, who was always around the village. Although not terribly bright he was usually friendly and helpful, especially to Brianna.

She found him in the village where he was tending the garden in front of the school. "Paul, can you help me please? I want to make a memorial for Clarissa."

"Clarissa? Oh yes, your sister, have you f-found her?"

"No Paul that's why we need to put up a memorial, some stones."

"What's a m-mem-moriable?" stuttered Paul.

"It's like a headstone," said Brianna.

"What, like in a ch-churchyard?"

"No! No, somewhere else,"

"What place?"

"Well, I have found a special place in the woods by the stream and I want to set up some stones in a circle," Brianna told him. "But it's our secret."

"I can b-bring my Dad's pick, shovel and hand cart," Paul announced enthusiastically.

"That would be lovely."

It actually took them two weeks to get all the stones erected but by careful choice they now had a very respectable stone circle.

"F-finished?" said Paul, proud that he had helped Brianna and sorry that the game was over.

"No, we have to move one more stone from the cliff top but we'll do that tomorrow."

Next day, Paul and Brianna trundled the cart off to the mine head. It took most of the morning to extract the special pool stone and get it into the cart. The journey across the hills to the woods was very rocky and hilly, so it was almost evening by the time they arrived. They pushed the stone into the hollow they had prepared in the centre of the ring. Finally, the memorial was complete; even if was not magical it would always act as a shrine to her sister that would last forever.

"Thanks Paul. I could never have done it without you."

Bright and early next morning she set off for the woods with a small tin pail from the kitchen, hoping her Mum would not notice it had gone. She arrived at the circle and realised she had chosen the place really well. The sun was sparkling off the dew, giving it a wondrous glow. She vowed to find more bulbs like bluebells and daffodils to add to the crocuses and snowdrops, to ensure that every spring in the glade would be a joy to behold.

She fetched some fresh water from the stream and filled the pool stone before casting a few petals over the surface. She had also brought a small spike with her to prick her finger. She stirred the water with her hand, mixing the blood and petals, and watched them swirl around the pool.

"Clarissa, can you find your circle?"

The petals slowly circled but there were no words forming.

"Clarissa, please answer me."

There was no response and Brianna was very sad. She lay by the river and a few teardrops rolled down her cheeks as she thought that all the hard work was for nothing. Eventually she drifted off to sleep in the warm sunshine.

An hour or so later she woke to a magical sight. There, in the reflection of the stream and the pool, bright sparks of light seemed to be dancing across the grass and dipping in and out of the pool. She had never witnessed nor experienced such joy and passion before. She watched for over an hour before the vision faded and all was quiet again. She walked over to the pool and saw the sign written in the petals, 'Thank you. We love you B.'

Once again tears rolled down her cheeks but this time they were tears of joy. She vowed that one day, when she was older, she would create a bigger ring to give the Sprites more freedom.

One fine spring day, Brianna went back to the stone circle and to her delight the glade was a profusion of flowers. She sprinkled flower petals once again and shared some blood with the water. There was no immediate response. She lay down on the bank and watched the sparkling sun and in a light sleep, dreamt of Clarissa.

'Look in the pond,' Clarissa commanded.

Brianna woke with a start and walked over to the pond.

'You have now opened our world to the outside. Thank you B.'

The words seemed to run across the water and Brianna felt she could hear them as well.

The water started swirling around gently and when it subsided Brianna clearly heard Clarissa's voice.

'We are now able to roam more freely through the woods and fields although we are still tied to the circle.

'We hope to expand our talks with the living and maybe one day we will be rescued. Keep us in your heart always.'

Chapter 9 – Caught in the Act

"Stop thief!" came the cry from behind her.

Damn, she had been seen, time to run. Racing from the village towards the woods determined not to be caught again, she leapt over the small stone wall, thankfully landing well, on the turf beyond the rocks. She raced across the open field, with her pursuer not far behind, thinking that if she could reach the edge of the woods, maybe she could evade the hunter.

At least dressed as a boy, Brianna was not hampered by a flowing dress. Looking back, she realised he was gaining. She threw a stone she had been carrying for such a situation, not her best move as she almost tumbled, but it had the desired affect. He tripped when he ducked to avoid the missile and fell hard. This gave her time to reach cover of the trees. It was time to make a stand as there was little chance to outrun him. Readying her sword and hiding behind a stout oak she waited until she heard him stumbling through the gorse and heather before leaping out and taking a huge swipe with her sword.

But again, he had stumbled and the weapon swished at empty air. He quickly recovered his ground and began his concerted attack; she parried his blows, managing a few strikes but was forced backwards through brambles and undergrowth. So, fierce was his attack that she fell over backwards having taken glancing blows on her legs and arms. He fell on her, his sword forcing its way to her throat.

"Time to die!" he shouted triumphantly, as the blade reached her skin.

"Pax! Pax!" cried Brianna.

"Give up then Bryan," gloated John.

"Yes, yes, you've won, again," said Brianna.

"You need to strengthen up Bryan," said John, standing up.

She wasn't going to tell him who she really was or their games might be over. She always dressed in boys' garb when she came to St. Erth, trying to trace Jan's progress. She knew that he had moved up north of the county and on her trips, had found a companion in John, who always had the latest information.

"You need to build up your muscles, Bryan," he told her, but not unkindly. She had told him she'd lost her father and he assumed that this was reflected in her lack of stamina.

They sat on the hill overlooking the town. "So, what's the latest gossip John?"

"Mrs Peterson has got a new lover."

"Thanks John but I want to know about Jan."

"You're obsessed with him, aren't you?"

"He took something from my Mum and I want to get even."

"You'll have a job to get one over on him. I hear he's taken over the smelter now so he's becoming quite powerful."

"Where does he get his money?" Knowing full well, that Jan had had virtually nothing when he left the mine. Maybe he had made more money than he had told her Mum when he sold the mine or had bullied his way to riches.

"No idea but rumour has it that he blackmailed the original owner."

"I wouldn't put it past him," said Brianna. She had come here to try and trick Jan into revealing what had happened so she could expose him. "I must go, see you next week."

"Bye Bryan."

Brianna made her way home nursing her aches and pains from the game, but one day she might need the strength and skills she gained from their sparring matches.

Brianna stopped off to pick up some berries that she had stored yesterday. She had told her Mum that she was off picking fruit and whilst she didn't like telling fibs she preferred that to explaining what she was really doing.

A few days later she went to visit the glade to see if she could contact Clarissa again. She had made regular visits to keep the area clear of weeds and saplings as well as planting an ever-increasing circle of bulbs and flowering plants. Occasionally she would call up the sprites and enjoy their frolicking in the sunshine but it always left her sad when she had to leave.

Her contacts with Clarissa through the medium of the pond had been sporadic, merely talk of what she was doing, the frolics of the new spring lambs and what was going on in her world. Clarissa developed with her, in terms of language and knowledge.

One day the discussions took a more serious turn as Brianna told her of her suspicions of Jan.

'That's who it was,' spelt Clarissa.

"Who do you mean?"

'I remember now, it was Uncle Jan who took me away.'

"I always knew it was Jan but could never prove it."

'You have to stop him.'

"He is much too strong and powerful for me to stop him."

'You must use your art and the skills of your hands to expose what he has done.'

"I promise I will never let him get away with it but it will take time and guile," said Brianna. "Somehow I will find ways and means to make his life miserable. He will never enjoy the riches if I can help it." A big promise and although in her heart she doubted she would be able to deliver on it, she had to try.

'I will help where I can but you need to make me

stronger and visible in the minds of all people,' spelt Clarissa.

"How will I do that?"

But the connection with Clarissa, always tenuous, drifted away and Brianna was left with her thoughts. How would she keep the spirit of Clarissa alive? All she had was the skills of her hands and brain. That was it of course, she had always enjoyed doing things with her hands and drawing was a skill she had had from a young child.

Maybe that was it; maybe she could bring the spirits alive through her art, pottery and poetry. She would lift up the imaginations of children everywhere to the joys and pleasures that the spirits could bring to their lives. She would try to convince people that there were magical, powerful and protective spirits, giving comfort to their grieving, joy to their living and peace to those that had passed on. Maybe even use art to denounce Jan. Brianna walked home with new resolve.

"What have you been up to today Brianna?" asked her Mum. "You seem very happy"

"It's been a lovely day and I've decided to make some money with my pots."

"Pots? There's not much money in pots."

"There will be in mine, well maybe not a lot, but enough to bring in a bit. It won't cost much as I've found some lovely white clay in the hills. Then maybe I'll paint some pictures for the locals.

"I'm not convinced Brianna; I might be able to get you a job in the house you know."

"Maybe Mum, but once I start that I would never get out of it, but if the pots don't work out we can talk about it." No way was she ever going to go into service. She had more ambitious plans, being 'in service' would never give her the freedom she needed to exact revenge on Jan.

Brianna didn't have a potter's wheel so she had to start by making coiled pottery. Using a brown clay base and then decorating them with whiter clay she could fashion some beautiful designs. Now her problem was firing the pots.

She had made friends with a young lad from the village named Trevan, who earned a living making charcoal from the coppiced woods.

"Trevan, I need your help," she said to him one morning, using his obvious attraction to her, to her advantage.

"I will if I can."

"I need to fire my pots and the only person with a kiln is miles away and would charge a fortune."

"What do I get out of it?" he asked blushing furiously, feeling he may have overstepped the mark.

"Money of course, we can share the profits." Brianna showed him some of the lovely pottery she had made and managed to convince him that they could make money as soon as they could fire them.

Trevan agreed. "We will need some bricks and clay to make the kiln."

"There's an old down farm shed near here. We could use the old bricks," said Brianna.

Transporting the bricks and building the kiln took many days. "I think that should work," said Trevan, standing back to admire their work.

"Is it ready to fire up do you think?" asked Brianna.

"I hope so. You get your pots and I'll get the charcoal ready."

She stacked up her pots carefully into the kiln hoping she had worked the clay sufficiently to remove air bubbles. She knew that one bad pot could reduce the whole lot to rubble.

"Ready?" asked Trevan.

"Fingers crossed," agreed Brianna, silently praying to Clarissa and her friends for a successful firing. "If this fails I shall be down in the scullery."

They lit the fires and using the bellows they built up the temperature to the right level. Taking turns on the bellows to maintain the temperature for most of the day, they prayed that their hard work would pay off.

"I'm exhausted," said Brianna, as they woke up the next morning to a beautiful dawn chorus.

"Who's Clarissa?" asked Trevan. "You were talking about her in your sleep."

"My guardian angel I hope," said Brianna. "No, she is my sister who was abducted years ago."

"She said she had been helping with the pots."

"I'm sorry?" said Brianna, confused.

"You were talking in a strange little girl's voice, she said she would make sure your pots would be fine."

"Really? Well I must admit I had some strange dreams last night but didn't know I talked in my sleep."

Plucking up courage and holding their breath, they started to open up the kiln.

"These are amazing Brianna," said Trevan as they revealed the startling pots.

"They really have come out well," she said admiring the colours she had created. "There must be a lot of minerals in the clay to make them glow like this."

"There's a few that broke but generally most of them have survived," he said.

The heat had created unexpected colours and had transformed the simple pots into beautiful works of art. Pretty spirits dancing around the circumference in white clay gave the pots a life of their own. Brianna knew that if her pots could be properly glazed in full colour and maybe with gold inlay, they would be even more beautiful, but that would cost money.

The next day they loaded the pots onto Trevan's cart and set off for the market. They laid them out on the ground and Trevan went back to his woods, certain that his charcoal coated face would detract from their wares. The pots were not only pleasing to the eye, they were both unusual and practical. Brianna was delighted to have sold all but one by lunch time.

A burley man came bumbling over. "Do you have a license to sell here, young girl?"

"No, never heard you needed a licence."

"Of course, you need a licence. I will have to fine you all your takings," said man gruffly, leaning over with more than a simple menace.

Oh no thought Brianna all her takings for nothing. "Everything?" she said, close to tears.

"You can't come here and sell your wares without paying fees."

"That's not fair."

"Life's not fair. Now pay up."

"Ed! She's on my patch, now leave her alone," came a voice from the shop door.

"What!"

"You heard, now leave."

Ed mooched off, annoyed that his attempt to extort her money had failed.

"Sorry about that. He's right you know, you do need a licence. But your pots have drawn a good trade to this corner and I've done well today."

"Thanks for helping. Sorry if I'm on your space," said Brianna.

"No problem as I say it's been a good day for me as

well. You attracted quite a crowd. Let me have your last pot."

"Please take it."

"No, I insist on paying for it," said the man. "My name is Jeremy."

"Brianna," she told him, pointing to the jewellery shop, where she could see his workshop behind a small display of exquisite jewels. "Is this your place?"

"Yes, probably a bit upmarket for such a small town but I get by," said Jeremy. "So, do you have many more of these pots?"

"This was the last of this firing but I'm going to make more," she said.

"Well Brianna, I think you are onto a winner here, can you have some more ready for next Friday?" asked Jeremy.

"Of course. Friday?"

"Market day, again," he said. "Well bring them over and I'll put a stall outside."

"What about Ed and his licence?"

"I'll sort that out and you can pay me a small percentage for the space."

"I'll see you on Friday then, bye."

Brianna rushed back to Trevan with the good news.

"I think we will make more money doing this than selling charcoal," said Trevan.

"Yes, but without the charcoal we have nothing." She gave him a grin and wanted to give him a hug as well, but felt that maybe it was not appropriate.

"Once we have enough money put by, we can build new kilns and also start properly glazing them," said Brianna, brimming with enthusiasm.

"So, how did it go?" asked her Mum that evening when she returned from work.

"Wonderful, I sold everything and there's even a shop that wants to display my pots."

"So, where's mine then?" she teased.

"Share of the money or you can have this little figurine I made for you," presenting her Mum with a tiny angel. Brianna had painted her in a bright purple outfit using juices from the fruit she had collected.

"Oh, darling it's lovely."

"It's so that Clarissa is always with us."

"I'll put it in the window so she catches the sunshine," said her Mum, small tears glistening on her cheeks.

"One day I'll be able to glaze it properly."

_____

"So, what do you think Trevan," said Brianna, holding up her latest creation.

"Amazing but will it sell?"

"Of course, trust me I'm a potter," said Brianna. "I suppose an artist these days." Brianna's reputation had grown across the county and together with Trevan's and Jeremy's help, her works were in demand in both small homes and large country houses. True to her word to Clarissa, she concentrated on ethereal scenes depicting woodland sprites, fairies and traditional Cornish pixies, and her work had become immensely popular.

She had learnt the art of appealing to people's hearts rather than ordinary plain and practical pottery. She had also progressed to beautiful glazed china, once Trevan had managed to build a high temperature kiln.

Brianna married Trevan after much persistence from him and they adored their four children, Reginald the eldest; followed by the twins Charlie and John and finally a bubbly daughter, Beatrice. It was only after Beatrice was born, did Brianna feel the need to confide in Trevan about her suspicions of Jan and the fears for their daughter.

"Trevan, you can understand that now that we have Beatrice, we need to be more vigilant than ever," said Brianna.

"Why, you don't think he would try anything around here, do you? He's long gone surely," said Trevan, once he knew the background of Brianna's lost sister.

"I think he still keeps an eye on his old mine. I have been following his activities over the years you know."

"So that's where you go on your foraging trips."

"Now Trevan, don't get uppity, most of them are foraging for new materials but I have a friend in St. Erth who keeps me up to date."

"Does your friend fancy you?"

"Trevan! Since when were you jealous," she teased, giving him a hug. "I doubt it, he knows me as Bryan. I used to play with him when we were younger."

"So why do you think Jan may still be coming down here."

"I think his wealth is intricately linked to the mine, even though the mine itself is not operating."

"Maybe we should check it out one day, see if we can unravel the mystery."

"It's very dangerous Trevan, I'm not sure it's worth the risk," said Brianna. "We will need keep a proper look out though."

Brianna continued her occasional visits to the pool, often carrying Beatrice when the weather was warm. One day her peaceful existence was shattered when Clarissa sent a message.

'The Borgats are getting excited'

"Borgats?"

'Monsters of the caves'

"Why are they excited?"

"Fresh blood coming'

"What, a new girl?"

'Think so, you must save her'

Brianna raced home.

Chapter 10 – Power Corrupts

"What are you looking at, stealing back your money?" accused Jenna.

"You don't need it, witch," shouted Jan.

She came at him holding a wickedly curled knife. "I know what you're up to." She growled, slashing at his body and drawing blood from his chest.

Jan grabbed her arm, he had been in too many fights to succumb to an old woman. "You'll pay for that."

He pushed her down on the dirt floor and tied her arms together.

"Get off me. I'll get you into prison."

"I doubt that," he said, tying her legs together and dumping her onto the bed.

"My spirit will come after you," she threatened.

Jan, fresh from his vision in the church, hesitated but then knew he had come too far to stop now.

"I should have sorted you out earlier. Now where do you keep that foxglove preparation?" he asked looking through the small pile of potions.

"Get away from me or I won't tell you what was on that knife," she shouted.

"Even if you had put something on the knife, I expect you have an antidote somewhere in here," he spat back.

He grabbed her and poured what he hoped to be a poisonous liquid down her throat, before she had a chance to stop his attack.

He held her head back as she gurgled and spluttered, desperately trying to avoid swallowing. She thrashed and convulsed as the poison entered her body. She finally went limp on the bed, as her heart gradually gave way. He untied her and laid her to rest in her bed as if sleeping. He finished his search, retrieving some of his money and her potion book, before quietly leaving the scene of the crime, worried about the tingling sensation across his chest.

....

"Did you hear about my mother?" asked Jan's Solicitor, Edward.

"Jenna? No, why what happened to her?" asked Jan, feigning ignorance although the festering chest infection kept reminding him of their altercation.

"She died in her sleep apparently," said Edward. "She wasn't found for a couple of weeks after she died.

"Shame, she was such a good teacher," said Jan. "I hadn't seen her for some time."

"Well she would live in that old hut in the woods, otherwise she may have been found in time to help her," said the Solicitor. "Never mind, she was a good age I suppose. Now what can I do for you today?"

"I think it's time for me to make a Will, don't you?" asked Jan, happy to avoid any more questions about Jenna.

"Certainly, I'll draw one up."

"I want to leave everything to my eldest son, I assume that's normal."

"Yes, perfectly standard, if you come in tomorrow, I'll have you something ready to sign. How's the venture with Mr Treagrove going?"

"Excellent, thanks to you for spotting those sneaky clauses," said Jan. "However, I need to change their business model if I am going to make a lot of money, but we can discuss those options in a few weeks when a few other pieces of the jigsaw have fallen into place."

"Only a pleasure to help, Jan."

"As long as there is something in it for you," said Jan.

"Well that would help of course," said Edward.

Jan's new-found skills had a major bearing on his future when Mr Treagrove had a sudden heart attack. Treagrove's new Will left his business interests to Jan. Despite a family challenge and with the help of Edward, the Will was upheld and Jan was set for life with a legitimate business to explain his wealth.

******

Jan soon expanded the business, selling off the interests in mines in exchange for coal imports and transport, to take control of the profitable side of the business. It would take time to reap the benefits from the business but he was desperate to show off his wealth. The best way to achieve this would be to buy or build a country home. There was always a price to pay for his greed and Jenna and Mr Treagrove had certainly paid the ultimate price. But he only had one source of guaranteed quick riches. It was time to pay a quiet visit to Mrs Jones and her sets of twins, she certainly wouldn't miss one of her daughters and after all, she had enough of them.

Once considered, it took no time for Jan to put the plan into action. He never enjoyed the visit down the mines but it was all in a good cause, his own of course.

He travelled down to the south coast and met up with the widow ostensibly to find out how life was treating her.

"So, Mrs Jones how are you coping?" he asked when he arrived at her home.

"Oh, hello Jan," said Mrs Jones. "Not well I'm afraid. Bringing up four children is not the easiest even with the money you paid us."

"I do have a solution if you are willing," he said.

"And what solution is that?" she asked.

"Well my wife is pining for another child and unfortunately can no longer bear any children," he lied.

"That's very sad," said Mrs Jones.

"We could take one of your younger girls off your hands and bring her up at our expense," he explained.

"I'm not sure about that."

"She'll have all the advantages we can give her and my sons to protect her."

"I'd miss her terribly."

"You'd still be able to visit her, of course," continued Jan. "And I could give you a small sum to help with the rest of your family."

Finally, after a long discussion the deal was completed and after a surreptitious visit to the mines, Jan soon had a new pouch of jewels.

Once back home he called in the local Architect.

"I want something grand and imposing as befits my new station in life," said Jan, as they toured the farm he had bought.

"Modern or traditional?"

"What do you suggest?"

"You're not from a family line of country gentry, I would say something modern. Good straight lines but imposing, I would think. I'll draw something up for you."

"I cannot visualise flat drawings, I insist on a scale model, can you do that?"

"Certainly."

******

"What's your problem, Greg?" asked Jan.

Greg, the foreman, had burst into Jan's office at the smelter works. Jan had groomed Greg from the time he had met him at the pub, not because he liked him but he needed someone he could manipulate who would also intimidate other workers with his huge build.

"Your son is getting too big for his boots, I want him off the foundry floor," said the surly foreman.

"What's he done now?"

"He tried to countermand my orders and I'm not having that."

Jan was secretly pleased that Gerald had attempted to stand up to this bully. "What happened?"

"I took him down a peg or two. No doubt he will come snivelling to you."

"What would you suggest Greg?"

"Give him an office job and keep him out of my hair." Greg thought he had a good relationship with Jan, after all he had been introduced to Jan's widowed sister-in-law Marion and they had a nice family going.

"I will talk to Gerald, oh and Greg."

"Yes."

"Don't ever burst into my office like that again."

Greg suddenly realised that he had overstepped the mark. "No. Sir."

Jan considered his options and decided it was time to reveal some plans and history to his son and considered that this was the opportunity he had been putting off for some time.

Later that evening he called Gerald into the study of their new home.

"Lock the door behind you."

"Yes."

"Yes sir." Gerald realised that this was not going to be a good meeting.

"It's time for you to understand your duties to the family and our heritage, but also for you a time for revenge. I understand you tried to stand up to Greg but lost out."

Gerald hung his head. "Yes, but he didn't fight fair."

"Winners rarely fight fair, let that be a lesson to you," said Jan, secretly please that his son had a least tried to stand up to the bully. "However, sometimes the direct approach against bullies isn't always the best. I have a different way for you to get your own back."

Gerald tilted his head. "Really?"

"You may wonder where we got our head start in business from, the humble miners we once were."

Gerald had a vague recollection of the tiny hovel they had lived in when he was a small child.

"There was an accident in the mines which my brothers and I owned. Actually, it was more an altercation with some underground creatures."

"Creatures! What sort of creatures?"

"Don't interrupt. It's a long story so I need you to listen carefully. These creatures provided jewels and gold in exchange for some favours, more specifically providing them with small children."

"What for?"

"I don't want to know but think it's about their blood. Now we have to honour my commitment otherwise we will be back in poverty, or worse," continued Jan. "There is an obligation to provide a child of the family blood line in exchange for more financial rewards. This is why I have kept in touch with the family and supported them where necessary, even to the extent of getting Greg to marry Marion."

"But I thought we were already rich, why do we

need more money?"

"I am in the process of buying into some Welsh smelters in Swansea so I need the money quickly. Our smelters are too small to produce the pure copper that is in demand so I will soon be closing this operation once the new smelters are operating."

"So that's my revenge, having Greg out of work? Not much satisfaction there."

"No, your revenge will be to spirit away his young daughter."

"Do you mean kidnap Aimee, are you serious?"

"Completely. Do you have a problem with that?"

"Sounds perfect, when should I get her?"

"The second lesson for today is patience and cunning, not brute force. We must not be suspected in any way or we will be finished, and be under no illusion, that if it's only you that gets caught I will deny any knowledge of your act. Do you understand me?"

"Yes sir."

"So, I can trust you implicitly."

"Absolutely."

"Good, if this goes well I shall be able to appoint you my manager in Swansea. I'll need someone close to me to look after the investment. Now we need to make a plan of action."

Some days later they met up at the entrance to the mine, Gerald burdened with a sack of the writhing Aimee. Jan showed Gerald the hidden entrance and how to avoid the tricks, traps and deceptions.

"Gerald, I want you to spend a couple of weeks setting more complex devices down here, I want this to be a dangerous place for anyone that tries to get in here."

Aimee was still struggling even in her bound

condition. "She's a right little fighter isn't she," remarked Gerald.

"All the better," agreed Jan.

There was the sound of dislodged stones falling into water behind them.

"Did you close the entrance properly," asked Jan quietly, "Idiot child, go back and check, we don't want anyone following us."

Chapter 11 - Brianna in the Dark

"Trevan, Trevan where are you?" called Brianna as she rushed into their home.

"What's wrong?" asked Trevan, appearing from the back.

"There's a problem down the mine."

"You haven't been down the mine have you, I told you not to do anything without me," he scolded, taking hold of her shoulders.

"No, no, but Clarissa tells me they're waiting for a new girl."

"Who's waiting?"

"The Borgats."

"Brianna you're not making sense, come here." Trevan's arms welcomed her trembling form. "Now tell me what happened."

"I was at the pool and Clarissa told me that the Borgats were expecting some new blood. We need to stop it."

"We can't watch every child in the county, Brianna."

She slumped down realising the enormity of the challenge ahead. "No, but we could keep an eye on the mine entrance for a couple of days."

"Fine, but let's get the children over to your sister," said Trevan.

Putting their home in order, they bundled up the children and took them to the family, with strict instructions to keep them safe and together at all times.

Brianna and Trevan sat behind some stone walls overlooking the mine workings. Their surveillance efforts were helped by the overcast day but there had been nothing to see. After a long and cramped day and about to trudge home, they were distressed when they spied not one, but two hunched figures walking furtively across the moor.

"Keep down Brianna," whispered Trevan. "It could be nothing."

Brianna dropped down but kept her eyes on them. One figure was carrying a large sack over his shoulder. A cold chill made Brianna shudder with horror. Terrified that the sack contained a child, she whispered in Trevan's ear. "We have to do something."

"They're too far away," said Trevan.

"We could shout and chase them off."

"They're armed, Brianna," said Trevan. "Didn't you see their flintlocks sticking out of their belts? We'd be dead before we had a chance to overpower them."

"We have to try though," said Brianna.

"We have only one chance to rescue her, if indeed it's a girl they have with them, is by stealth."

They watched as the men opened the entrance and disappeared into the mine tower.

"Strange, I thought you said it was blocked off," he said.

"It was," said Brianna. "Quick let's get down there and find the way they entered."

Now that they could no longer be seen, they raced towards the mine head hoping that something could still be done for the girl.

Surprisingly, the entrance had been left slightly open and Trevan carefully looked inside. A contraption hanging over the entrance looked extremely dangerous but a rope held it in place.

"Come on we have to follow them," said Brianna.

"Yes, but take great care, these caves are very dangerous. I think I should go on alone," whispered Trevan.

"No Trevan, I'm coming with you, don't argue, now get on with it."

They lit their small candles and seeing a ledge around the inside of the mine entrance, Trevan eased his way around, towards the sounds and dim lights ahead, followed by Brianna.

Gaining the entrance to the next tunnel proved difficult but voices drifted back to them.

"Son! What's that noise? Hey you idiot, did you close the entrance?"

"Sorry Dad,"

"Get back there and make sure no-one followed us and that the entrance is closed up. Can't I trust you to do anything?"

"On my own? Ow, that hurt."

"Yes, you stupid child and if you don't go now you'll get more than the back of my hand, now go."

Brianna pulled Trevan back into a tiny alcove hoping this was their chance whilst the two were separated. She could hear the son stumbling back along the cave towards their hiding place.

Brianna could feel Trevan bracing himself ready for an attack. As the lad passed, Trevan gave him a swift punch to the stomach, followed by a chop to his neck, flooring him. Brianna grabbed the lantern from his hands before he fell, avoiding a crash that would have alerted the father.

Trevan was about to tip the limp form over the edge, but Brianna didn't want his death on her conscience and stopped him, tying him with his jacket instead.

"Now for the father," whispered Trevan. "You stay here."

"Come on son, hurry up," called the father.

Trevan grunted a response, hoping that he would get an opportunity to surprise the father. Brianna watched from a dark corner as Trevan crept forward.

A bright flash lit up the cave and a huge explosion reverberated around the caverns. A scream came from Trevan as he was thrown backwards. How Brianna managed to restrain herself from shouting out she never knew.

"Well, who do we have here? Never mind I'm sure the Borgats will have some fun with you." said the man.

Not knowing whether Trevan was alive or dead, Brianna slunk further into the corner and snuffed out her candle, not wanting to suffer the same fate.

"Where's Gerald?" asked the man.

"Gerald?" Trevan groaned, so at least Brianna knew he was still alive at this stage.

"My son, what have you done with him?"

A thump and another scream from her husband.

"Is he dead?"

"No," came a feeble reply, followed by another kick and groan.

"Well, you soon will be."

The man reappeared and found the bound form of Gerald lying a few feet from Brianna's hiding place.

"Are you alright, stupid child, getting caught like that," asked the man, releasing his son. "Come on, get up we have to finish this."

"Let me kill him Dad," the son pleaded, trying to make up for his failure.

"No, drag him with us and we'll feed him to the Borgats."

Brianna regretted her decision not to tip Gerald over the edge, but it was too late now. Determined to try and save Trevan and if possible the girl, she carefully followed the two as they dragged her unconscious husband and the hessian bag through the caves.

Peering through the darkness, she saw father and son had stopped at a dead end in the cave. They started clearing the rock fall and exposed an entrance to the cavern.

"We are here as promised, with another of the blood line," called the father.

He held up his lantern, which lit up the cave and started climbing down.

"Good God. What are those?" asked Gerald.

"Sad to say, they were my brothers who were taken before I had a chance to negotiate their release."

"I thought you said they died in a rock fall," said Gerald.

"Don't believe everything people tell you."

Leaving their bundle on the floor, they clambered back to safety.

Brianna saw a small form leap up and dive at Gerald.

"God's blood!" cried Gerald.

"What was that?"

"Her damn cat, she wouldn't let it go, bloody thing scratched my face."

"Well it won't last long down here," said the father.

Brianna held out her arms and the small cat ran to her and they cuddled up in the dark corner.

"I'm glad you kept your bargain," growled a deep voice, reverberating throughout the depths of the cavern.

There was a tremendous crashing and scratching from the depths of the cavern. Brianna cowered in her corner wondering how she would ever have a chance against so many.

"I suppose you want some more trinkets?" came the deep voice. "You are such a treacherous and despicable little man. Who's that with you?"

"My son, Gerald. He will be keeping up our agreement in future."

"Are you as wicked as your father? Never mind, I expect you are," he growled. "Give them their rewards."

Brianna heard a thud and crash of coins and trinkets.

"Now let's close this tunnel."

Brianna heard them replacing the rocks.

They were putting the last rock to fill the hole, when a duet of voices floated up from the depths. "We're following you."

"What was that?" asked a fearful Gerald.

"Nothing! Now let's get this finished."

The final rock in place and the father gave some final instructions to his son. "Right Gerald, you close up the caves and reset the traps," he said. "I have to get back to business before I'm missed."

"But Dad!"

"Shut up and whilst you're at it, get rid of that," said the father, kicking the now inert form of Brianna's husband, before quickly passing her hiding place, oblivious to everything but his money.

She peered out to find Gerald dragging Trevan towards a sheer drop. Now was her chance she thought; her hand had been unknowingly, resting on a block of wood. She held it in her hands and charged at Gerald, swinging it at his head, but he turned towards her at the sound of her feet. However, there was a still a satisfying crack as she knocked him clean off his feet.

She knelt down to check Trevan's pulse and could feel nothing. "Oh Trevan. What has he done to you?"

"I'll give you 'oh Trevan'" said Gerald, standing over her, blood streaming from his face, aiming a kick with his big boot. Brianna rolled away from his foot which caught her arm. The cat leapt at Gerald, digging its claws into the cut on his face, pulling the skin away. Gerald screamed, trying to detach the cat, eventually throwing it off.

He raced off. "Good luck down here. I'll leave you to rot in this hell hole for eternity," he shouted.

Brianna heard the sounds of a trap door slamming down somewhere in the distance.

Chapter 13 – Trapped Forever

Brianna fell to the ground, weeping for her lost husband. She had no idea how long she remained there sobbing and grieving but noises from the depths of the cave brought her back to reality with a start. Something was definitely moving around down here. She sat up realising that she needed to get out of here for her children's sake and maybe exact her revenge before she could grieve. Her arm still felt numb from the boy's blow, but gradually the feeling returned, to be replaced by sharp pains.

Picking herself up, she stood against the wall and began to slowly feel her way back down the tunnels. Holding her body as close to the wet wall as she could, she moved away from the blocked exit. Her hand slipped into a cavity as she inched along. Her fingers felt some stones and a coin. Maybe she could use the stones for a distraction if she needed it. Images of paying the ferryman with the coin briefly flashed through her mind before continuing.

One step at a time, she shuffled forward trying to remember what she had seen before the lamps had been extinguished. Hours went by as she struggled higher and higher towards the surface.

"Think positive thoughts," she said out loud. Hatred drove her forward. The sound of distant running water drifted from the tunnels. She thought a drink would be a good plan and coming across a small stream she had a drink which refreshed her body and mind. It was almost her undoing as she slipped on the rocks and almost fell in. A thrashing sound assailed her ears. That doesn't sound good she thought, backing away from the stream. How would she ever get out of here? Exhausted, she sat against the wall and drifted into a restless sleep.

When she woke she saw a dim light shimmering from a tunnel she had failed to see earlier. Vague memories or dreams came back to her, of someone calling 'Follow me!' Faint from a lack of water but with nothing to lose, she pulled herself up and decided to head for the light. Could this be the way out? Carefully she followed the dim light picking out features, avoiding obvious plunges into the depths. Rounding a corner, the light grew brighter, tiny stars were shining down through a shaft above. The dim light fluttering in the cave still beckoned up ahead.

She reached the top of a rise of rough rocks and in her dreamy state tripped and rolled down the hill, words drifting into her mind, 'Revenge Trevan!' She could hear waves crashing onto a beach and feel the spray on her face. She stumbled along the beach in the dark, no idea where she had ended up, before finally collapsing in a heap on the wet sand.

Waking to the warming sun, no idea how long she had lain there, she made her way wearily over the hills, cautious to keep close to the stone walls avoiding contact with anyone who might be still on the lookout for her. She hoped her assailant had been scarred for life following the attack on his face; it would be the only way she would recognise him, should they ever meet up again.

She arrived home, the tiny mirror reflecting her hollow pale skin, drained of life. She needed to put on a brave face for the sake of her children, not sure she could achieve that today, but pinching her cheeks reddened them enough.

She headed over to her sister Mary's home to collect the children.

The door opened to her knock. "Brianna! Where have you been, we thought you were dead! You've been gone so long!" exclaimed Mary. "Come in, come in. I'll call the children. Is Trevan with you?"

"Sadly, Trevan is dead," said Brianna.

"Oh Brianna! What happened?" asked Mary.

Brianna related a short version of the story to Mary but told her not to pass the details on to the children.

"What are you going to do?" asked Mary.

"I have to get on with life and look after the children. What else can I do? There is no justice without proof," she replied, keeping her thoughts of revenge to herself.

"There's no easy way to say this but I am afraid your father has been killed on the cliffs," she told her boys once they were back home.

"How?" asked Charlie, one of the twins.

"We were searching for new materials when the cliff collapsed," she said.

Reginald gave her a hug. "I'm sorry Mother, but at least you are safe."

"Now children we are not going to be beaten by this," she told them. "Reginald, you are now the man of the house and I want you to try and take over from Trevan. I think if you can look after the charcoal production and boys, you can help me with the pottery side of the business. We can't afford to sit around and mope. Are we all agreed?"

"Yes Mum," they chorused. Brianna was thankful for Trevan's strict upbringing in such a difficult situation. Later, when getting ready for bed and removing her torn and dirty clothes, the stones she had found, fell out of her pocket, rattling across the floor, along with the coin she had picked up. It rolled across the floor, bouncing over the flagstones, glinting in the reflected candlelight, before disappearing under the bed.

She picked up the coloured stones then reaching under the bed, her fingers finally grasping the tiny object. Holding it in the light she realised she had found a gold coin. "Now this will come in useful," she said, admiring her find, hopefully this would help her recover from the disaster.

A few years later their struggling and hard work had bought the stability the family deserved but she still harboured the need to avenge Trevan's death. She could not prove who the attackers were but still kept her eyes out for the younger man with a scar.

"Morning Jeremy," called Brianna as she arrived in town to meet the jeweller, Mr Goldsworthy, where she still sold her wares.

"Morning Brianna. Now what have you got for me today?" Over the years her pottery and plates had made a considerable impression on the local people. "You certainly have the magic touch with your pottery. It's almost as if you knew what people wanted before they do." Jeremy often displayed her pieces along with his silver creations in the windows of his shop.

"Not too much sadly, my kiln is on its last legs and I need some cash to replace it," said Brianna.

"You know I'd do almost anything to keep the pottery business going but not sure I can fund something like that without some sort of security," said Jeremy.

"Oh, I don't want a hand out," said Brianna, "I have a coin that Trevan left me for emergencies, maybe it's worth something."

Jeremy took the coin and examined it closely. "This is definitely gold and very rare. Where did you say he got it?"

"He said it was from his father, who found it on the beach," lied Brianna quickly.

"Well I have a collector who would jump at this, excellent quality, a very lucky find. I'll take it to him today and see what he is prepared to pay for it. Certainly, it will be enough for a kiln."

"Oh, thank you Jeremy," she said, wanting to give him a hug but doubted it was the right response for a business transaction.

A couple of days later Jeremy called Brianna into the shop. "We were very lucky there, with the recent jump in gold price I obtained a lot more than expected so you can certainly get your kiln and more."

"Thanks Jeremy," Brianna said and this time did give him a hug. "Oops sorry"

"Uhh," said Jeremy, embarrassed. "That's alright."

They separated and Brianna looked down at the floor.

"I do however have a proposition for you," said Jeremy.

Brianna backed away, sure that she was going to be exploited and cheated out of her money.

"Don't worry! I don't intend to take your money. What I would like to suggest is that you join me in the business.

"Join you? I don't understand."

"Your insights into the desires of customers is increasing my business."

"I have feelings' that's all," said Brianna. "So, what are you suggesting."

"You can set up the kiln in the extension at the back of my workshop," he continued. "And in return I will teach you how to work in silver."

Brianna decided she couldn't refuse, especially with winter approaching. "Of course, I accept."

A loud exclamation came from the shop, interrupting her concentration of an intricate carving on her latest creation.

"What's the matter?" Brianna called out.

"I've lost the safe key," said Jeremy.

"Where did you put it?"

"If I knew that it wouldn't be lost," he said.

"Sorry, silly thing to say." Brianna came through to the shop and although they hunted the whole place, they had no luck finding the key.

"I remember what it looks like. Said Brianna.

"Maybe I can fashion something."

She spent the next hour making something similar to the key, but they couldn't quite get it to turn the lock. She made some adjustable parts, which involved inserting some of the components that she used for her new jewellery line. Despite the changes, it still refused to work in the lock.

"If I coat it with gold leaf, we can see where it's catching," she said.

"I hope you're right. Gold is expensive."

They painted some gold foil on the key and inserted the key into the lock. Brianna manipulated it, hoping that the marks the lock made would highlight the problem. She took it out and they could see where it was catching. A final small alteration and the safe door swung open.

"That's saved me a fortune on having to break the safe open and having a new one made," enthused Jeremy. "Well done!"

"That's alright. It was fun," said Brianna, always loving praise from Jeremy.

"Brianna this could be very useful in the future. I often have customers who have lost their safe keys and your tool would make our life easier when they do."

"There are a few adjustments it needs to make it more universal," she agreed, "but yes, I'm very pleased with it."

One sunny morning Brianna decided to visit the magic pool and once she had summoned Clarissa, she told her about the key.

'Show me' spelt Clarissa.

Brianna took out the golden key which glinted in the sunshine.

'Pretty - drop it in,' she spelt out in the petals.

Brianna dropped it in the pool, which started to

bubble and steam, before settling down and floating up to the surface again.

'Now I am one with the key and it will always be your friend.'

"Thanks Clarissa,"

'Now then, how about you?'

"Me? I'm fine," said Brianna.

'No, you're not.'

"Well it's two years since Trevan was killed," said Brianna. "And I still miss him so much."

'I know what you should do,' Clarissa spoke through the petals.

"About what?"

'Your life.'

"My life's coming together, thank you."

'No, you're lonely, it's time to move on.'

"Move on?"

'Yes, you've been working with Jeremy now for many years. I'm sure he has a soft spot for you.'

"Don't be silly, it's only a business partnership!"

'Maybe on your side, but I think he would make an excellent choice.'

"For what?"

'Marriage of course.'

"I can't, my heart still mourns for Trevan."

'Trevan thinks it's for the best.'

"Can I talk to him?"

'He's still in a dark place, hoping for revenge,' said Crystal. 'But he told me he wants to see you happy again.'

Over the next few months Brianna considered this idea. She was not convinced that Clarissa had it right, until one day when they were sitting in his workshop, Jeremy started talking. He stopped, stumbling on his own words.

"Sorry, what did you say, Jeremy?"

Gathering courage, he went on, "Brianna, you must know I have admired you for some time now."

"But……."

"Shush, let me finish before I lose my nerve. I think it's been some time since Trevan died and I know I can never replace him but I would like to try."

"Replace him?"

"Don't make this difficult Brianna."

"Are you asking me to marry you?" asked Brianna, as a warm glow filled her body.

"Well, you know all my secrets and you still have the key to my safe, so it's probably best that we make things formal. Your children accept me as a friend and I would like to be able to give you a more secure home."

"You know I still have a mission in life which may get in the way," said Brianna.

"I'm sure you are talking about resolving the issues following Trevan's demise but a task shared -," said Jeremy with a friendly smile.

"I'd love to, yes," said Brianna, smiling back before being smothered in his comforting arms.

Some months later, Brianna was working out in the back when Jeremy came through to see her.

"You wouldn't believe who came in and gave us a commission?"

Brianna's reputation had grown, specifically for her decorated china. True to her word to Clarissa, she had tried to promote the magical world of sprites by painting wondrous scenes of dancing fairies in mystical woodlands.

"Commission?"

"There is a bit of a social climber in St. Erth, who is desperate for a set of your china. All the plates and serving pieces for twenty place settings."

"That's huge, I haven't made a set that size before. I'm not convinced I can manage such a huge order!"

"Why not buy a standard set?"

"She wants a specific magical woodland design."

"I'm still not sure I can do it."

"I think you will when I tell you who she is married to," said Jeremy. "Your old enemy Jan,"

Chapter 14 – The China Talks

Brianna and Jeremy and the family laboured day and night to finish the commission. Brianna explained what she had put in the patterns and although wary, Jeremy agreed that it would have the desired effect. They finally took the trip together to the Garrett home. The butler, more like a thug that Jan had bought in to keep out unwanted guests, let them in with some specific instructions.

"Madam wishes that the table be laid out so she can get the full effect, follow me," said the butler.

They took the crates through to the dining area and laid all the china and silverware out. Four silver candlesticks adorned the middle of the table and a magnificent silver centrepiece depicting a Viking sailing ship finished the effect. The soup plates sat in the centre of the dinner plates, disguising the secret dancers and some of the gold pattern.

"Where's that butler? Hello!" called Jeremy, once they had finished.

"Yes sir?" said the butler appearing once more.

"Please tell Mrs Garrett that she can come in now."

Isabella entered the dining room. "Oh, that's wonderful, look at all the colours, such drama. My friends will be so impressed."

Hopefully, thought Brianna the more the better.

Isabella picked up a plate and examined it carefully. "Yes, it's perfect. I was told you were the best."

"There is the small amount of the bill still outstanding madam," said Brianna. They had already been paid enough to give them a profit, as they knew that by tomorrow getting more would be impossible.

"You will have to see my husband about that; he's

at the works at the moment. If you call next week he'll settle up."

"Thank you."

"Yes, I'm sure, thank you for your work. Now John, I don't want the dining table touched 'til the party on Saturday. Please see them out."

A rather perfunctory dismissal thought Brianna but they were happy to be out of this hateful house; well Saturday may bring some surprises at their party, she thought.

******

"Jan come and see," called Isabella, from the dining room.

"What?"

"The dinner set." Her bloody dinner set, she had talked about nothing else for weeks but it was in a good cause, he had invited some potential investors in his new project for a dinner party. Isabella may be demanding, but hopefully she would be a good hostess.

"I'm sure it's lovely," said Jan, "Hopefully the chefs will do an equally good job."

Saturday arrived and all the guests, some reluctantly, some greedy for an investment or a chance to beat Jan at his own game. After drinks and canapés, the butler announced dinner.

Having taken their places, the soup was served and consumed. Even Jan enjoyed the taste, so things were going well so far. Wine flowed and conversation was animated. As darkness was falling, Jan asked for the candles to be lit and drapes closed. Soup plates removed; and the pictures of dancing sprites in magical woods on the plates were revealed.

"Amazing," said one of the ladies.

Isabella glowed in the praise. Draughts from the open doors, as serving staff cleared the table, meant that the candlelight flickered and reflected on the gold inlay.

"Oh, look around the edge. How clever, it's writing."

"What is it?" asked another. "Some sort of monogram?"

The words glowed and shone. Finally, the guests deciphered the beautiful script, cunningly inscribed on each plate.

'Child Murderer'

Chapter 15 – Sleight of Hand

"I hear that the dinner party was a disaster," said Jeremy.

"Excellent," replied Brianna. "That's the beginning; I wish we could do something more damaging."

"I want you to be on your guard when you're out these next few days, Brianna," said Jeremy. "Garrett is going to be particularly aggrieved about the collapse of his standing in the community."

"Don't worry I'll be careful, we know how vindictive he can be," said Brianna. "But at least he won't get the support he had in the past."

"Yes, you can only buy so much loyalty," agreed Jeremy.

"Who attended his dinner?"

"Mostly local dignitaries and investors," said Jeremy. "Including the Justice of the Peace, Lord Trevarnoe."

"Interesting," said Brianna.

"What happens if he investigates the china set?" asked Jeremy.

"We'll have to cover our tracks, but I've already thought that one out." said Brianna, explaining what she had done.

"Very clever, in which case I'm looking forward to the visit," said Jeremy.

A ring of the front door of their shop a few days later heralded the arrival of the not unexpected Justice of the Peace.

"Good morning Sir," greeted Jeremy, pretending that he would be expecting another sale from the regular customer. "What can I do for you today?"

"I'm not here to buy today Jeremy," said the JP. "Something far more serious I'm afraid."

"Oh dear, not fake silver surely," said Jeremy.

"No, but I believe you delivered a china dinner service to the Garretts recently," said the GP.

"Correct."

"Well he has made a complaint."

"I thought they loved it," said Jeremy.

"At first yes, did you make it yourself?"

"No, my wife is the potter, shall I call her?" said Jeremy.

The JP nodded.

"Brianna, I need you out front."

"Yes, oh hello Lord Trevarnoe," said Brianna.

"I believe you made this china," said the JP, handing over the damning plate with the gold design.

"Certainly, looks like mine, why?"

"There is a serious accusation written on the plate," said the JP. "'Child Murderer' is written in gold."

Jeremy examined the plate, "I can't see it."

"Nor can I in daylight, but trust me when candles are lit, it is exposed."

"Really, let me get one of my copies," she said going back into her workshop, to collect the carefully prepared plate.

"Lord Trevarnoe, would you mind closing the curtains," said Jeremy, lighting a candelabra on the work top.

Brianna quickly switched plates once the JP's back was turned.

"Now let's see," said Brianna. "This is identical to the plates I delivered."

Try as he might the JP failed to see the words in the cursive squiggles in gold. "I can't see anything."

"Now let's see the plate you brought with you," said Brianna. Twisting the plate in the candlelight the words magically appeared.

"Oh dear," said Jeremy, feigning his horror. "What have you done?"

"Nothing," said Brianna, seemingly scrutinising the plate. "Look, Lord Trevarnoe can you see the different gold colours."

"Indeed."

"Let me use a cloth on the plate," said Brianna, briskly rubbing the plate.

She held up the cloth showing traces of gold paint and the plate returned to the original meaningless squiggles.

"Something's really odd going on here," said Jeremy.

"Do you think the Garretts deliberately overpainted the plates?" said Lord Trevarnoe.

"It certainly looks like it, I wonder why?" said Jeremy.

"Well either the wife was accusing her husband for some reason or Jan was accusing the dignitaries around the table of some crime," said the JP. "I'm glad that's cleared up as far as you are concerned, never liked that upstart Garrett."

"Maybe he was trying to involve us some sort of scandal," said Brianna.

"Maybe," said Lord Trevarnoe. "It will certainly be worth an investigation."

"You'll keep us out of it."

"Of course, goodbye."

"Goodbye."

"Well done Brianna that was brilliantly done," said Jeremy, giving her a big hug.

Chapter 16 - Manacles in the Dungeon

Their business flourished over the winter months, no doubt as a result of the patronage of Lord Trevarnoe promoting their shop to rub salt into Garretts wounds. Success meant they were working extra hard to produce the china and silver desired by their clients and left little time to ponder on the threat from Garrett.

"We have to deliver this china today Jeremy," said Brianna, one morning.

"We can't. I have this centerpiece to finish," answered Jeremy.

"I've promised, anyway it's only local."

"Well, just be careful then," said Jeremy, absorbed in the complexity of his work as he grappled with the intricate silver ornament.

Drifting in her thoughts, on the misty spring morning, using the small pony and trap around the countries lanes, meant she missed the burly figure leaping onto her cart until it was too late. A dark sack engulfed her and tight ropes were drawn around her body before she even had time to cry out.

Low gruff voices reached her ears through the wet and smelly sacking. She screamed for help but her voice cracked and the sack, plus the damp morning muffled her calls. Who would hear her anyway, out here in the empty countryside but she had to try something. A strong hand clamped over her face stifling any more cries.

Stupid girl she thought, letting her guard down like that. She began to cry as she realised this could be the end of her life after all her efforts. What would her children do without her? Jeremy would be distraught if she couldn't get away and he wouldn't be looking for her until late that day. Somehow, she knew this wouldn't end well.

She felt the sack tighten around her face and she was thrown into the back, jarring her body on the crates of china.

"Get out of 'ere quick."

A crack of a whip and the frightened pony galloped off down the track. Brianna felt every jolt and bump as her body tried to absorb the jolting in the back of the cart. A particularly deep rut bounced the cart so much, that a crate of china bounced out the back and smashed onto the road, leaving a trail of broken plates down the track. All her hard work destroyed, but that was probably the least of her worries.

"Slow down, stupid," growled one of the men. "You'll have us all off, then we'll be for it."

Brianna hoped the other man would listen. Mind you, maybe falling off might be preferable to her imagined future, at least it would be a quick death. She tried rolling around and sitting up but she realised that she was wedged between the last two crates. Gradually the pony calmed down to a walk and for the next hour or so Brianna despaired of any chance of escape. The jolting disturbed the ropes around her face.

"Help! Help me!" she shouted, no idea if anyone else was on the road. The cart pulled up and she was lifted bodily and struck around the head.

"Shut up, stupid woman, or we'll chuck you in the river."

Another rope was retied around her head and pulled tight, and she could taste the damp filthy sack as it was forced between her teeth, effectively gagging her from all but muffled cries. Was she always going to be at the mercy of a megalomaniac with no conscience?

The cart finally came to a halt and she felt strong arms lifting her up. Brianna cried out as was roughly manhandled off the back of the cart and slung over a shoulder. She tried kicking her assailant but it had no effect. She heard his footsteps crunching underfoot before the creak of a door opening and her legs banging on the door frame and walls. Finally dumped unceremoniously on a cold floor, the sack ripped off and her hands grabbed.

Her arms felt as if they were going to be ripped out of her sockets as the two men pulled her upwards and she felt manacles clicked onto her wrists. Too shocked to scream before, she now spat and ranted at the two men before one took a rag once again and shoved it roughly into her mouth. Brianna tried to discern the faces of the men in the dim light from the door but apart from the huge nose on one as he was silhouetted in the door frame, she could make out very little. They slammed the door shut behind them leaving her in total darkness.

Brianna slumped to the floor defeated for now but not yet beaten. How would she get out of here? She put her head down between her knees and managed to get the filthy rag out of her mouth and called out. "Help! Help!"

Her voice sounded flat and she realised that no sound would emanate from this deep cellar. "Why, oh why did I reawaken Jan's wrath?"

Many hours later the door of her prison opened and a dim light from a flickering lantern, revealed a dark room, a cupboard in one corner and a simple writing desk against one wall. Brianna quickly scanned the room whilst she had a chance, looking for any likely exit. The damp walls and flaking white paint, confirmed to her that this room was underground which held little hope of another way out. Black metal implements hung from the wall, definitely not simple mining tools, more like instruments of torture.

"So, little girl – Brianna, isn't it? All grown up but still making my life difficult," said her Uncle Jan, advancing towards her.

"Leave me alone, you brute," she shouted.

"I'm afraid that's not going to happen," he sneered. "You haven't learnt your lesson yet."

"Do your worse, you've taken the best things from my life anyway," she said, with a bravery she didn't feel.

"Oh yes, did you ever find Trevan's body, or what was left of it? How did you get out of there anyway?"

Brianna glared at him, the memory of her murdered husband still haunting her.

"Never mind. You will find my dungeon a little more difficult to escape from, I expect."

"You can't hurt me anymore."

"Maybe. Well, there are still your children of course. You should have left well alone."

"Never!"

"Stand up. Let me look at you one last time." His hard, pockmarked face filled her vision. He pulled her up by her shoulders. Brianna stared at him, trying to be brave and attempting a kick but he was too quick for her.

"Still some fighting spirit, I like that, all the more fun in breaking you," said Jan. "I always thought you were going to be trouble and I should have dealt with you earlier."

Jan picked one of the ancient tools of torture from the wall; a wicked looking head mask, with inward pointing spikes where the eyes should be. "Now the question is, would it be the eyes or the tongue that should go first?" he said, removing a vicious set of pincers from the wall.

"I'll tell you what. I'll let you choose, shall I?"

"You're mad," said Brianna, not able to take her precious eyes off the mask.

"I'll leave these on the table here so you can make your choice whilst I'm away," he said, moving a small table in front of her and dumping the objects on top as well as a small lantern glowing over the objects, creating even more frightening shadows on the dirty white wall opposite.

"I always think that the thought of torture to come, is more excruciatingly than the reality, don't you? You'll be able to tell me tomorrow."

Jan turned, opened the door and Brianna quickly screamed for help.

"There's no-one to hear you down here, so save your breath."

"What about your wife? She can't be happy to be married to a monster like you."

"Wife? Oh yes she didn't last long down here, not into torture apparently."

Jan went out of the dungeon, chuckling to himself, locking the door behind him.

Brianna slumped down to the floor again and burst into tears.

Chapter 17 - Miners Materialise

Brianna awoke from a fitful sleep, her arms and legs aching from their restricted positions, hoping that her incarceration was only a dream. Despair engulfed her once more as she rattled the manacles helplessly, but as long as she was alive there was always the smallest chance of getting out of here. Jeremy would be out searching for her no doubt, even coming to the house but would quickly be fobbed off by the scheming Jan.

'Are you trapped?' said an eerie voice. 'And why all the tears?'

"What?" said Brianna looking up, expecting that Jan had returned, but the door was still closed.

'Are you trapped down here?'

Brianna could see nothing; no doubt some form of trickery or maybe a speaking tube.

"Yes," said Brianna, through her dry lips. "Who are you?"

'Jan's conscience.'

"I'm sorry, what do you mean?"

'Jan's conscience, but I'm not doing very well so far, am I?'

"No. Where are you?"

A figure of a skinny man, shabbily dressed in a dirty khaki jacket and an old felt hat of a Cornish miner, drifted into view out of the thick walls.

'Here,' the apparition said proudly. 'And who might you be?'

Brianna thought she must be hallucinating, probably a lack of food and water. She closed her eyes to try and clear the image.

'Who are you?' it asked again.

Brianna opened her eyes, hoping that the vision had gone, but it still stood in the corner.

"Are you still here?" she asked.

'Oh yes and who are you?' it asked again.

"Brianna."

'Brianna? I knew a Brianna once, a long time ago.'

"Are you also trapped here?"

'Sometimes.'

"How do you get out?"

'I simply imagine which part of the house I want to be in.'

"Well, I can't do that."

'No? But if I help you, will you help us?'

"Us?"

'Me and my brother.'

"Why can't I see him?"

'He's distracting Jan.'

"I don't see how I can help you," Brianna asked. Sometimes being a psychic played tricks on her mind, maybe playing along would help her cope with the situation.

'Of course,' said the apparition.

"Can you tell me how to get out of here," she asked, hopefully.

'You are the key,'

"That's not much help,"

'Key. The key you made.'

"Key? Oh key. Yes, good idea."

Brianna realised that she had been so shocked by the abduction and terrified of Jan that her brain had stalled.

'When you get out, will you help us?'

"What do you want me to do?"

'We need you to help us stop Jan if you can.'

"Stop him what?"

'He abducted a girl and if we don't stop him it will carry on for generations.'

"Clarissa?"

'You know Clarissa? But we don't think she'll be the last. Do you promise to help?'

"I cannot do otherwise. What are your names."

'I'm Tom and my brother is Mark or what's left of us.'

It finally dawned on her that these apparitions, or her own mind games, represented her uncle and father. So, could this could all be a dream. "You're my uncle?" she asked.

'Oh, you're that Brianna. I'd love to give you a hug but I don't think that that is possible,' it said, floating towards her.

"You were killed by a rock fall in the mining tunnels, weren't you?"

'So that's the story he put about. No, we were trapped by monsters and Jan abandoned us down in the depths.'

"Monsters?"

'You don't want to know.'

"So how can I help?" asked Brianna.

'Firstly, you need to get out of the house.'

"I'll try my best."

'Then you must disappear. You must go to your pool and call us.'

The voice fell silent and the apparition faded to nothing.

"Tom. Tom?" but it had gone.

Brianna stood up and carefully reached under the folds of her dress, not wanting to put a strain her sore wrists, and with a huge sense of relief, found her little lock picking kit. Hoping that Tom was right, then Jan would not be around for a time. Brianna's experience and the clever design of her master key made short work of the shackles. She rubbed her wrists where they had dug in.

Having got them off, she closed them up and relocked them. Looking around the room she found a discarded A-line dress on a shelf. She held it up and she realised from the bloodstains, that this may have belonged to his ex-wife. Not the time to feel squeamish, she quickly swapped outfits, then put the sleeves of her own dress through the shackles and draped it to the floor to give the impression that she had disintegrated. She inserted a pole through the dress and taking the wicked face mask, clamped it shut and wedged it on the top of the dress.

"That will give you something to think about, Jan."

She climbed the stone steps by the cellar door; the soundproof door meant she could hear nothing beyond it. She picked up a metal bar to defend herself, in case Jan returned.

She carefully inserted her key and with a few manipulations felt the lock give. Gently turning the key, there was a click as the lock disengaged. She waited behind the door listening for any movement. No sounds came through the tiny crack, so she slowly opened the door but was confronted by a blank wall.

"What now?"

Looking down she could see runners under the wall. Pushing the wall, it slid open slightly and she peered out through the small crack. The cellar opened up into a study with a red leather chair behind a huge desk; obviously Jan's study. Papers and drawings covered the desk no doubt some new devious scheme he was drawing up; long shelves packed with books around the walls.

Brianna turned and relocked the cellar door and slid back the fake wall of dummy book shelves. Brianna checked the curtains and could only see the dark night through the gaps; the clock in the corner showed 2.35, an excellent time to give her a chance to disappear without being discovered. She would have loved to search through the papers on Jan's desk but her first priority was to escape. The long drapes in front of the window rustled in a light breeze, pulling them open, she found a small window had been left open but offered her no way out. Peering out into the back garden she could see a group of large shrubs to cover her retreat, if she could only get out. Feeling something under her found she picked up a key lying on the floor.

She had to find a room with a door out to the garden but before she could explore the other rooms, she heard steps outside the study. Hiding quickly in the alcove behind the drapes she held her breath. The study door opened and Jan came in and sat down in the leather chair, the new leather creaking under his weight. Brianna held her breath from behind the curtains, dreading the moment Jan ripped them open.

Chapter 18 - Jan Loses It

Brianna heard Jan stand up and the chair rolling back against the cellar door. She held her breath thinking she had been discovered. If she was found now, Jan would not give her a second chance. She heard his footsteps as he circled the room opening drawers and slamming them back.

"Where's that damn key?" he shouted, before stomping out of the room and banging the door shut.

So that was the key she had found. Thank goodness, he had lost the key or she would have been discovered before she had a chance to get away. She emerged warily from behind the drapes and walked over to the door and looked out into the corridor. The flickering candle on the wall gave off an earie light but at least it was empty. She ran to the next door and went inside but it turned out to be just a linen closet, she heard the charging Jan lumbering around the hall and she quickly closed the door before he saw her.

Waiting for the din to subside, took all her patience. After what seemed like an age, she crept once more from the cupboard into the hall and luckily the next room was more promising. Faint lights reflected into the room through a French window. She raced over and with a quick application of her magic key, had the door unlocked and rushed out towards the bushes.

A light drifted through the house as Jan seemed to be searching for something, shouting at the staff as he went through the extensive rooms of the house. Curtains were pulled back in the study and a light shone out, but Brianna dived into the undergrowth and lay perfectly still until the light went out. She quietly crept away keeping in the shadows of the rhododendrons; then sinking down again as the curtains in an upstairs room were pulled back and a window closed. At last, as the house went quiet and lights dimmed, she began her long journey home.

Keeping to the fringes of the roads, desperate not to be seen, it would take her many hours to get there. The dark night slowed her progress as she tripped and fell over unseen tree roots, scraping her knees and hands, until the moon rose and lit up more serious obstacles, which could have been her downfall. She had no idea when Jan would realise she had gone and send out a search party. Once she heard a horse galloping across the moor and dived into the bracken, not wanting to be caught, even though she thought that it wouldn't be Jan. She arrived at the back of her home before dawn and quietly let herself in through the kitchen door.

Brianna felt the faint warmth of the huge black cast iron stove, as she crept into the comfort of her own home. No doubt Jeremy had been searching for her across the countryside and had forgotten to keep the fire going. She placed a couple of logs on the dying embers, filled the kettle and set it to boil, before slumping down exhausted, into her favourite rocking chair. Hopefully Jeremy would soon wake and they could plan their next moves.

"Brianna! When did you get back?"

Brianna jumped, startled out of her sleep. "Jeremy! Keep quiet... ssshh."

"I was about to come out and search for you again."

"Thankfully I'm home now, no thanks to Jan."

"What happened to you?" he whispered, as he brushed the moss and leaves from her hair.

"Jan's thugs grabbed me."

"And what's all this blood?" he asked, holding up the dress. "And where did you get this?"

"It's not my blood thank goodness."

"What happened?" he asked. "I thought your horse had bolted. We found broken china in the road, but no sign of you or the cart."

"Not bolted, no. I was attacked by Jan's thugs and taken to his house." Brianna proceeded to relate her ordeal, trying not to break into tears. She missed out the part that the apparition had played.

"I'm going to kill him," said Jeremy.

"Wait," said Brianna, hanging onto his shirt. "That's not going to work. At the moment, he thinks I'm still in the basement and when he gets down there, assuming he has a spare key, he'll think I'm dead or at least vanished. I want it to stay that way."

"Maybe you're right," said Jeremy. "But we have to find a way to punish him."

"I agree but I may have an idea," said Brianna, explaining the thoughts she had whilst hiding in the woods.

"I don't want anyone to know what happened and I definitely don't want Jan to know what happened to me. I intend to make his life hell but I can't do that if he thinks I am alive."

"Let's go upstairs then and make our plans," he agreed. "Let me get you cleaned up."

The next morning Jeremy came to Brianna's room, tucked away at the back of the property.

"Well, here's a twist," said Jeremy, giving Brianna a hot drink of honey. "I have been asked by one of Jan's thugs to sort out a locked room for them."

"Really, don't they know who you are?" asked Brianna.

"I'm sure Jan does and probably thinks this is the greatest irony to open a door where you are incarcerated," he replied.

"Or maybe a simple trap to throw you into the same cellar."

"Yes, but I am at least forewarned and can take precautions."

"Maybe this is an opportunity to get back my master key though," Brianna was annoyed that she had dropped it as she escaped from Jan's house.

"Are you sure you left it there?"

"Positive, I remember using it to open the French doors but not when I reached the bushes and I wasn't going back."

"I'll have a look before I go in."

"Make sure you get the special key first, in case they try and lock you in."

"Can't you make a new master key?"

"I can but it will take too long."

"If it makes you happier I'll take Reginald with me and keep a look out," said Jeremy. "Don't worry I won't let him inside the house."

"It's probably the only way he'll see what I've set up for him."

"Maybe a good fright of what he sees down there might keep him off our backs," said Jeremy.

Chapter 19 - Monsters in the Pool

Jeremy arrived at the estate early next morning and he positioned the cart behind a group of trees out of direct sight of the house.

"We don't trust anyone here," Jeremy said to Reginald. "Once you see me go inside, move the cart into a prominent position so that you are visible to anyone inside, but too far for anyone to creep up on you," instructed Jeremy.

"Yes sir, and take care yourself."

Jeremy walked down to the house going around the back through the stable area and finally reached the French window where Brianna thought she had left her key. A brief search revealed the skeleton key, concealed by a large flower pot and he quickly tucked it away under his jacket as he heard someone approaching from behind.

"Hey what are you doing back 'ere," said a gruff voice, as Jeremy felt his shoulder grabbed.

"I've been summoned to sort out a locked door and was looking for the tradesman's entrance."

"Well, it's not here," said the burly man. "Come with me."

Half directed and half dragged to the kitchen door, Jeremy found himself in the large sunken kitchen.

"Wait here."

Jeremy stood in the cavernous kitchen, watching the maids as they scuttled around preparing a variety of breakfast dishes. The delicious smell of bacon and devilled kidneys, made him realise how far Jan had come from his humble beginnings. No wonder Jan was so protective of his new lifestyle.

"This way," said the red-haired guard.

Jeremy followed the big man through the house, ending up in the study where Jan stood, still in a foul temper, no doubt still feeling thwarted by the locked door and deprived of his longed-for torture of Brianna. Jeremy shivered involuntarily.

"Don't I know you?" queried Jan as he pulled back the fake shelves of books.

"I don't believe so," answered Jeremy, hoping that Jan didn't realise his relationship to Brianna.

"Really?"

"Positive."

"Anyway, can you get in here?" he asked, revealing the safe door.

Jeremy went to the door and took out the tools from his travel box. "It won't be easy, this is a complex lock, but I should be able to get in. It may take some time."

"Fine. Red, you stay here don't let him in there, I don't want my jewels stolen."

The big man nodded, "Yes boss."

Jeremy set to work on trying to break into the cellar door, laboriously fitting and filing and with sighs and curses pretending that this job was more difficult than it really was, hoping the Red would drop his guard. After a couple of hours, Red was starting to fidget.

"How much longer?"

"I've made the dummy key," said Jeremy, standing up awkwardly, stretching his legs. "Take me to Mr Garrett."

Red turned and went out of the room giving Jeremy the chance to glean some of the details of the paperwork and maps on his desk, before following him out.

Red led Jeremy out to the dining room where Jan was waiting impatiently. "Well?"

"I've fashioned a temporary key in soft metal, and will make the finished product at the shop. If Red comes to the workshop this afternoon he can collect it."

"Fine, as long as I get my key."

Once back at his shop Jeremy worked on the key in the back room actually just copying the original that Brianna had picked up.

A ring on the doorbell announced the arrival of Jan's bully.

"Here you are Red, and give your master the bill."

Once Red had cleared the house, Jeremy went upstairs to see Brianna.

"Have you done it?" she asked.

"Yes, I hope he gets the fright of his life when he gets in there," replied Jeremy.

* * * *

"I need to go to the magic pool one last time," said Brianna to her daughter Beatrice, a few days before they moved out of the area to their new home.

"Why mummy? I was hoping to complete my pots today."

"They'll have to wait, I'm afraid," said Brianna. "There is someone you need to meet, who may help you cope with your talents."

"Talents?"

"Your sight, understanding of the unknown."

"I thought they were just bad dreams," said Beatrice.

"Some dreams no doubt were. But you have the magical touch of creating pots that customers need as soon as their finished."

"I only imagine what people want."

"Before they even realise it," said Brianna. "I thought it was time to introduce you to some wonderful friends. The Sight has good and bad sides to it and you will need to know how to control your powers."

"Will I be able to cast spells?"

"It's not that sort of power Beatrice, although that would be a useful power sometimes," said her mother.

When Beatrice came back with her cloak, they hid their faces, crept out the back way, and out onto the moors.

"Beatrice, you know we are having a problem with the Jan, up at the big house," said Brianna, as they walked across the desolate moorland.

"Are they the ones who ordered the china?"

"Yes, but the problems with him go back to my childhood, which is why I need you to be prepared."

"For what?"

"For anything he might try and we will need as many friends as we can muster."

"That sounds scary."

"I don't think so, the sights I will show you are quite friendly if treated right. Firstly, we are going down to the stone rings."

"Sights?"

"We are going down there to meet my friend Crystal and maybe some others of the spirit world, who we will need to help us with the fight against Jan."

"Crystal, who's that? Do I know her?"

"More like a what, Crystal is the spirit of my sister and is now the guardian of the stones, my window into the world of lost children."

"Children? Does that mean there is more than one?" Beatrice asked.

"I think so sadly. Crystal has become my fighting spirit to help me in my battles."

Emerging from a small wooded area, they reached the magical fairy ring, set within in the flowering Hawthorn, wild roses and spring bulbs.

"It's beautiful?"

"Yes. Crystal instructed me to do it. Watch and you will understand. Collect a few flowers for me."

"Aren't these spring flowers?" Beatrice said, as she plucked a few of the petals.

"Oh yes, strange, isn't it? Now spread them over the pool."

Beatrice gently floated the petals across the surface of the dark blue water.

"Now, collect a rose stem."

Beatrice broke off a flowering rose.

"Ow"

"What's wrong."

"Oh, caught my finger on a thorn."

"That'll help with the last step," said her mother. "Now squeeze some blood in the water."

Beatrice squeezed her thumb and a few drops of blood fell into the water.

"Stir the petals and blood."

Beatrice dipped her hand into the warm water and began to gently stir the petals around and around in the sparking sunshine. The water in the stone hollow began trembling and bubbling, then boiled up furiously. Water sprayed both of them as two huge forms leapt into the sky.

Chapter 20 - Lion Dogs Attack

Beatrice screamed and fell into her mother's arms and they both leapt back, as the forms loomed over them dripping water and blocking the sunshine.

"Get off you brutes," shouted her mother.

"What are they mother?" cried Beatrice, clutching her mother's dress, hiding her face and shaking uncontrollably.

'Free! Free!' the images screamed, as mother and daughter tried to stand and flee, stumbling over each other.

"Tom, Mark!" called a gentle high-pitched voice from within the mists over the pool.

'What?'

'Get down here, you've frightened them,' said Crystal.

"Oh, sorry," said the two images, as they settled down.

'Sorry Brianna they just got over enthusiastic,' said Crystal.

"Who are they Mum?" asked, the still cowering Beatrice.

"The pretty one is Crystal, my long-lost sister," said Brianna, reassuring her daughter.

'And her father and uncle,' said Crystal.

"Not very people, more like monsters," said Beatrice. "They're so frightening."

'Sorry we frightened you. We'll come back later,' said the two forms, as they slowly faded into the pool, leaving Crystal in all her brilliance.

A white, gold and silver gown, adorned Crystal's ethereal body, with the sunshine glinting through the quartz gemstones, sending rainbow shafts across the already vibrant clearing.

"Wow she's beautiful," said Beatrice, peering from behind her mother.

'Thank you. Hello Brianna and who's this?' asked Crystal.

"This is my daughter Beatrice. I thought it was time you met."

'She's lovely.'

"Thank you."

'Welcome to my world Beatrice.'

"Are you a queen?" asked Beatrice, sure that the queens of fairy tales would look like the vision in front of them.

'No but it's nice to dress up.'

"You are very pretty Crystal."

'Thank you,' she said, giving a curtsey.

"Crystal, why doesn't Trevan come and see me?"

'Who's Trevan?' asked Crystal.

"My first husband."

'Shall I see if I can find him?'

"Yes please," said Brianna. "Meanwhile, I need to talk to my father Tom and my uncle Mark, could you get them back but more gently this time," said Brianna.

'Wait here, look into the pool.'

Crystal disappeared into the pool. Little rings of waves flowed across the surface. When they flattened out two male faces peered up from the depths.

"Father?" queried Brianna.

'Hello Brianna, yes sorry we got so excited before.'

"You gave us a fright," said Beatrice.

'We're glad that you managed to escape Jan before he really laid into you and you ended up like us!' said her father.

"Thank you for reminding me about the key."

'Thank you for opening this door for us,' said her ghostly father.

"Has he been down the cellar yet?"

'No, he's been away all day.'

"I would love to be there when he opens the door."

"You're not thinking of going to his house again, Mum?"

"I may have to."

'I'll help you,' said Crystal, reappearing. 'Trevan is still pondering his future, one day he may appear but he tells me you have to find a way to make him repay or at least repent for what he has done to all of us,'

'Knowing Jan, I don't think he would ever repent his actions, but we can certainly try to get him to repay us,' said Mark.

"What does Trevan suggest," asked Brianna.

'He said you need to put paid to any business plans he has, then maybe he can also find release,' said Crystal.

'Not sure I know how,' said Brianna.

'He suggested maps before fading away. Does that mean anything.'

"Jeremy saw some maps when he was in the house I'll ask him."

'So how can we help?' said her father.

"If I have to change the maps, it'll take me some time and maybe you can distract Jan," said Brianna.

'What if we drive him wild by spooking him?' said Tom, with an excited look on his image!

"Can you do that?" asked Brianna, hopefully.

'We don't know, we haven't tried it yet, we've been too miserable to do anything before.'

"You must try," said Brianna. "You were scary enough earlier."

"Crystal," called Beatrice. "You must know his secrets."

'He poisoned his first wife"

"How?" asked Brianna.

'Drugged her with a mushroom concoction, and then threw her down a well,' said Crystal. 'Would that help?'

"If we can get some proof."

'I could show you where.'

"Probably not enough to convict him," said Brianna. "He'd say it was an accident."

"What a nasty horrible man," said Beatrice.

'I don't think his second wife fared any better,' said Brianna.

'If he put her in the same place, I don't think the magistrate could ignore two bodies," said Beatrice.

"Maybe you could find out, Crystal," said Brianna.

'I'll try.'

"We'll we see you later," confirmed Brianna.

'You can count on us.' said Tom.

The clouds drifted across the sun and the apparitions drifted from view under the water.

"Oh, they've gone," said Beatrice "Lovely friends, scary, but wonderful, especially Crystal."

"Yes, she's lovely," said Brianna. "Sorry the miners scared you I didn't realise they would be there."

"So, they were your father and uncle," said Beatrice. "What happened to them?"

"A mining accident, according to Jan, but they tell me different. It's a long story, I'll explain on the way home."

When they got home, avoiding the centre of the village, they sat down with Jeremy to talk through last details before the big move.

"Jeremy, I saw Crystal. She's lovely." Beatrice burst out.

"Beatrice!"

"That's alright Brianna, I sort of realise what goes on down at the pool, although I still don't understand it," said Jeremy.

"Sorry Mum," said Beatrice.

"That's alright love."

"We're all ready to leave," said Jeremy. "The boys are prepared to take over duties in the shop and pottery, whilst we move to St Austell and start again."

"Hopefully it will be out of sight out of mind for Jan," said Brianna. "I need to go up there once more to put some final spikes in his game plan."

"No way, Brianna, said Jeremy. "I'm not letting you go back in there, it's too dangerous."

"I got out when he knew I was there and he still thinks I'm locked in his basement," said Brianna. "Anyway, I have no intention of getting caught!"

"Alright," muttered Jeremy, "but I will wait outside with the dog just in case. If there is any hint of trouble, blow this dog whistle and he'll will react and I can come in and get you. There's no use in arguing, otherwise I won't let you go."

"Fine, we'd better get ready," agreed Brianna, having realised she might need Jeremy's back up anyway.

"What do you want me to do?" asked Beatrice.

"You have to stay here and if we are not back by dawn, get the boys to storm the place."

Brianna packed her last remaining clothes ready for tonight's visit journey.

"I'm not sure about your trip to the house tonight," said Brianna, from the doorway.

"Have you had a premonition?"

"Not a bad feeling, but not a good one either."

"Why don't we try and contact Crystal and see what's going on?" said her mother.

"I'm too tired to go all the way to the pool again."

"I thought we might try together and create our own window to her world, here."

"I'll get some stones and a cup," said Beatrice.

Brianna took out her cards and when Beatrice returned they made a ring of stones and put the cup of water in the middle.

Brianna spread the cards in a typical cross style, and called for Crystal but nothing seemed to work.

"Wait," said Beatrice, and dropped a few petals from a posy in her dress.

Brianna took a needle from her sewing box and pricked her finger, stirring the peals. A spark flew out of the cup and lit up the room and Crystal appeared as a tiny water sprite, dancing in the cup.

'Hee Hee, I'm full of glee, opium in his tea, no knowing what he'll see,' Crystal chanted.

"Have you done it already?"

'Oh yes, he'll never know what hit him, but you have to go tonight as agreed. Not sure how long his visions will last.'

"Thank you, Crystal. Are Tom and Dad ready?"

'Oh, you just wait to see what they have in store for him. I have never seen them so excited!'

"Tell them I'm on my way. I can't wait to see what they have planned," said Brianna, as Crystal disappeared.

"Beatrice help me clear this up," she said.

Brianna donned the torn maid's clothes that she had worn the previous day. Armed with only her key and her wits, and of course hopefully her new-found friends, she and Jeremy stalked off to Jan's home.

Once they were near Jan's house, they dismounted the trap and tied the horse up.

"Pity we can't get closer" said Jeremy. "We could have made better time."

"Yes, but we would have been heard," replied Brianna.

They eventually arrived at Jan's mansion. It appeared even more imposing and threatening in its darkened state. There was no moon to light their way but their eyes were accustomed to the darkness and it was easier for them to get close to the back of the house without being seen.

"Now be very careful sweetheart, I don't want to lose you."

"I've got a few tricks up my sleeve," murmured Brianna.

"Don't forget the whistle now," said Jeremy, stroking their dog.

A quick hug and Brianna crept towards the back door, guessing that Jan's servants wouldn't bolt their only access to the house. She put her special key to the door lock and with a few deft movements, unlocked the door. Not only was it unbolted it was obviously kept well-oiled and opened easily and quietly. Brianna slipped in and closed the door behind her.

She sensed rather than heard someone behind her, and spinning around she was confronted by two snarling monstrous dogs, huge fangs dripping with slime. She fell backwards and slid down the door to the floor, stupefied by the images in front of her, their grotesque heads shaped more like lions than dogs, with long claws flexing out of their massive, hairy paws. Sharp claws that could rip her in two, fangs that could rip her throat out before she could utter a sound.

Thinking her time had come, Brianna pushed back up the door, trying desperately trying to reach the handle without success. Holding her foot up in a last act of defiance she searched for some sort of weapon, but she only had the small pen brought with her. Tears formed as she realised this plan had gone terrifying wrong. Why had she thought she could defeat Jan and his cohorts on her own.

She had not seen any dogs on her previous visits and she wondered where Jan had found such creatures. They were both very strange and seriously dangerous at the same time, and as her eyes got more accustomed to the darkness watched the bright red eyes glinting between dark green lashes. Slime was dripping from elongated fangs.

Reaching for her whistle to summon Jeremy to come to her rescue, but to her added horror, she realised she had dropped it when she spun around and could see it lying at the feet of one of the slathering dogs.

Chapter 21 - Haunting Jan

Closing her eyes and waiting for her fate, she heard a whisper in her ears.

"Oh, it's you Brianna" said one of the monsters.

Brianna opened her eyes to reveal the transformation of one of the monstrous heads into the gnarled face of her father.

"We were just trying out new ideas for haunting Jan, what do you think?" said the other ghostly form, Uncle Tom; her 'friendly' spirits.

"I was terrified! said Brianna, her heart still thumping away. "Thankfully I didn't scream or that would have given the game away."

"Sorry."

"That's alright but it was very impressive nevertheless. I loved the dripping fangs."

"That was my idea" said Tom. "I know Jan hates snakes,"

"Right I need to get into his study, do you want to go back to being dogs, just in case anyone is still awake."

The spirits changed back into their dog-like forms and together they crept through the house to get to Jan's study. The dogs melted and disappeared through the closed door and then, peering back through, they confirmed. "All clear."

Brianna checked the door, locked of course, but it was just a moment's work to open it with her master key. Closing and locking the door behind her, she saw that the ghost dogs were now sitting either side of the desk like brass Chinese statues.

"So that's where you got the idea," said Brianna.

They floated away from the statues. "Yes. Very clever we thought, being haunted by one's own statues. We are hoping that he'll start thinking that everything in the house might come to life."

"I can see you are going to have fun," said Brianna. "Right, stand guard as I need to go through his papers to try and understand what he's doing."

Briana studied the maps and traced the features with her finger, as she recognised the countryside that she knew so well. She recognised the roads and streams as well as the local farms. A dotted line ran across the map from the north down to the coast.

"What's this I wonder?" asked Brianna.

"Maybe trains," said a ghostly voice, over her shoulder.

"Don't do that," said Brianna with a start. "Why trains?"

"We've heard him muttering about trains," said the ghost.

"Maybe this is the idea he's trying to sell to investors.," said Brianna.

"Can you change the plan?" asked her ghostly father.

"Maybe, but how?"

"Add a river."

Now that would give the investors food for thought.

Brianna took out her fine pen and carefully extended the lines of the river right under the path of his railway. Another bridge would probably put all his calculations out. She carefully copied some of his 'investment' figures to show to Jeremy. Hopefully this would serve to destroy his financial plans.

'I think we need to improve the experience for Jan in the cellar,' said her ghostly friend.

"Why? I need to get out."

'But Brianna we want to try out our new powers.'

'It'll only take a second,' said the other ghost.

"Fine," said Brianna. "But we must be quick."

Brianna found the secret catch that revealed the entrance to the cellar. Using her key, she opened the door. In the light of the lantern, the tableau she had left before, had a flat look to it and had no depth. The dress just looked slack and the metal torture facemask hung down limp and unthreatening. Looking around there were a few rags in one corner and she started to stuff the dress to give it more 'body'.

'Still doesn't look real does it,' said Mark, floating past her.

"No."

'I have an idea.'

The clothes started to fill out as he took on Brianna's shape within the dress. The facemask lifted up and rested against the wall at an awkward angle.

"Very realistic," said Brianna. "What about some legs?"

'Legs?'

Brianna lifted her skirt to show what she meant.

'Oh yes legs, don't have much use for those,' said Mark and legs appeared under the dress.

"Maybe you should put them in the leg irons," said Brianna who despite the seriousness of the situation had to suppress a giggle at the splayed ankles.

'Better?'

"Much."

'He'll never know,' said Mark. 'Until he tries to touch me, then I'll turn into Medusa.'

"Heavens that will give me nightmares," said Brianna.

'Especially with Crystal's potions.'

"Oh yes I'd almost forgotten about that," said Brianna, turning to leave, locking the cellar door behind her and sliding the shelves across.

"Quiet, hide" whispered Tom, as the noise of footsteps rattled through the door from the passageway outside the study. Mark and Tom dissolved back into the brass lion-dogs by the desk. Brianna again hid behind the curtains.

The door swung back on its hinges, hitting the wall with a resounding bang before being kicked shut once more.

"Another investor pulled out," he shouted. "That china has almost ruined me but it's time for my revenge on that damn potter."

Brianna held her breath, frightened that he might start searching the room before they could spring the surprise. She hoped that his anger, induced by Crystal's drugs, would be sufficient to numb his mind to reality.

"Now where's that new key?" said Jan. "Better work or I have him down here as well."

Brianna heard him rifling through his papers and opening drawers.

"Ha ha, here you are," he said jingling the key. The chair fell over backwards, as he stood up sharply. Brianna heard the fake bookshelves sliding back.

Brianna heard him fumbling with the key until there was a loud click.

"Excellent. I must compliment him on his excellent work. Now for his wife."

Brianna trembled at what might have happened if she hadn't escaped, as she peered out from behind the curtains as he descended the steep stairs into the cellar leaving the study in darkness. She tiptoed across the carpet past his desk.

Peering into the gloom below, she watched as Jan dumped the lantern on the table.

"Now my beauty, have you decided what you would like to try first," he said, picking up one of the black instruments.

Mark had filled the skimpy dress and even she had to admit it looked real.

Looking up, Jan saw the metal face mask on her head. "How did that get there, I don't remember doing that?" He ripped open the mask. "I hope you haven't spoilt my fun."

Brianna's ghostly faces appeared from behind the mask, blood oozing from the eye sockets, the backs of the eyes protruding from the spikes in the mask.

"Serves you right but why you spoilt my fun I don't know."

The face started to change as yellow pus poured out of the empty sockets. Curly red hair breaking free from the head and starting to writhe and wave in the air. The black curly hair transformed into writhing snakes, mouths gaping and fangs dripping with poison, darting at Jan, getting closer and closer to his face.

Jan screamed as twenty snakes, fangs extended and hissing menacingly, reared their heads and started striking at Jan's face.

"Snakes! What the hell is this?" as one snake almost connected with his cheek.

Hell indeed, thought Brianna, as Mark, and his Methuselah images, extended the snakes' heads closer and closer to Jan. Brianna backed away and took up her usual hiding place, as Jan ran up the stairs to the exit. Tom had moved one of the brass lion-dogs in his way and he tripped and banged his head on the desk.

He swore again and screamed as he turned to find the dogs looming over his prone body. He grabbed at a brass poker by the fireplace and swung the sharp instrument at the forms passing straight through their ethereal bodies. Leaping up he shouted at the swirling forms. "Back off. Get out of here."

The brothers dropped their disguise and towered over Jan.

'Hello Jan. Remember us?'

"You're dead," said Jan. "Get out of my mind." He backed away from the cloudy figures.

But the ghosts were not finished with Jan yet and before he had time to recover, the lions re-appeared, snarling and hissing and dripping green slime from their fangs. They reared up on their hind legs trying to claw him open with their extended front paws. Jan raced out of the room slamming the door behind him.

Brianna emerged from behind the curtain to be greeted by the grinning images of Tom and Mark. "So how was that?" asked the ghost of her dad.

"Wonderful, you even scared me and I knew what was coming" said Brianna. "I think he'll avoid the cellar in the near future. I must go or Jeremy will be breaking the front door down."

"Bye!" they chorused, as she let herself out, down the hallway and out of the kitchen door.

Chapter 22 –Beatrice Deceived

"Wake up sleepy head."

Beatrice groaned as she turned over, stiff from the lumpy mattress, waking up after a fitful sleep at the inn, where her parents had stayed after their flight from Mount Bay.

"Why did we have to leave our comfortable beds?" asked Beatrice.

"You know that we have to keep out of the way of the Garrett family.

"Yes, but I didn't know how traumatic it would be," said Beatrice.

"A few bed bugs and straw mattress is a small price to pay to for our safety and a better future," said her mother.

"I'm sure that the old mattress contains the world's population of bugs and creepy crawlies," said Beatrice, scratching her itching skin, trying to relieve the irritations.

"I'm sorry darling," said Brianna, stretching to try and iron out her own stiffness. "I admit that was pretty unpleasant. We'll have to boil up these clothes as soon as we can."

"Can we get a hot bath here?" asked Beatrice.

"I ask the hotelier," said Jeremy. "But we probably need to find somewhere better, to be honest. Meanwhile I'll go into St. Austell and see what business opportunities there are."

Beatrice and Brianna went to see the owner to see what facilities there were.

"Can we get a hot bath here?" asked Brianna.

"You must be crazy," said the old man scratching and belching "Don't have any hot water 'ere. You gonna pay or what?"

Beatrice looked at her mother and they silently agreed to get out of here as soon as possible. Paying up and going out to the cart, Brianna called out.

"Wait Jeremy, we're coming with you."

"Good idea," said Jeremy, looking back at the scruffy hotelier standing in the doorway.

Beatrice and her mother sat on the overloaded cart as Jeremy led them into St Austell. They were rolling through the cobbled streets, shaking their belongings in the back when Jeremy exclaimed.

"Brianna, look at this." pointing to a 'For Sale' sign in the window of a local jewellers. "Stay here, I go in and have a look."

A few minutes later he emerged, "I can't believe our luck, this place is perfect, we'll put the cart around the back and we can all have a look."

Brianna stepped down from the cart when they reached the back courtyard. "This is huge," looking around at yard complete with outbuildings and stables, "perfect for my pottery business as well."

"I think we have come just at the right time. The silversmith is retiring due to poor eyesight. He is willing to sell us his shop and stock for a good price."

"Doesn't he have relatives to leave it to? It's unusual for someone not to have heirs in this age." Brianna queried.

"True. He had two sons but they were both lost during the Napoleonic war. His wife has long since passed on and this is a good opportunity for him to sell his business and for him to retire"

"There must be a catch," said Beatrice.

"I can't see one but let's go inside and talk to him," said Jeremy.

A few years later the business was thriving as St Austell became a hub of the business trade route from Cornwall to Devon coupled with the growth of the china clay mines. It had taken them only about 6 months to get settled into the new premises. Beatrice's mother had started to develop new techniques and styles in the pottery and china offerings, with Beatrice's help.

"Why do you paint so many dancing sprites, Mum?" asked Beatrice one day, admiring the latest china plates to come out of the kiln.

"I made a promise to your aunt and her spirit friends to keep their memories alive," she said, "and anyway the country people like a bit of fantasy."

"Except of course the Garretts," said Beatrice, remembering the tale.

"Yes well, we don't talk about them anymore. Hopefully they won't find us so far away from their country house."

Beatrice and Jeremy spent most of their time in the front of the shop and open workshop whilst her mum tended to keep out of the way in her pottery at the back. Beatrice worried about her mother as she became more reclusive as the years passed. She rarely ventured out in the streets and even then, used to dress up in drab clothes that hid her face.

Beatrice meanwhile busied herself with her own creations as well as presenting all their wares in a fabulous window display. Instead of the usual display of crowded items she had run themes, typically based on events or period settings. Her most successful displays included a spring woodland theme showing examples of sprites in both china and silver; a fairground display when the local fair was in town; to formal dining layouts, including china food on plates. These displays brought considerable attention and of course new business, it also brought a lot of attention to Beatrice herself, many people crowding around her latest conception. One young man in particular had taken a liking to her. Beatrice was intrigued and flattered by the attention he gave her. He remained a mystery, turning up on an irregular basis but always on the first day on her new window.

Plucking up courage one day she accosted him. "Excuse me but do you have spies that tell you what going on in our shop?" she asked, as he appeared one day, staring at the tableau.

"I do get to know when the next one is being prepared," he admitted.

"Do you live locally?"

"No but I have to visit St Austell occasionally."

"What just to see our window."

"No mostly on my father's business."

"Which is?"

"Oh, this and that," he said. "Down here it involves the china clay mines."

Beatrice used to look forward to his visits wondering and if it would ever lead to anything serious, hoping it would.

Her mother sat her down one afternoon, following one of his visits. "Are you keen on this young man then Beatrice?"

"Luke? He's very polite,"

"And good looking," said her mother.

"Well yes there's that as well," Beatrice said, blushing furiously.

"What do you know about him?"

"I know his dad is involved in business with the china mines and Luke comes down here on his business."

"And to see you?"

"It seems so."

"Well, be careful, that's all I can say."

"I will Mother," said Beatrice. "I think he may want to marry me."

"You are still young to make such a big step," said Brianna. "I'd be happier if you'd wait at least a year."

"Yes mother," said Beatrice, not telling her that Luke was already making plans for a quiet ceremony. Probably best to keep it a secret now that her mother had made her thoughts clear.

Her mum had always been over protective following the run-ins with the Garrett family, but there had been no untoward activity they had heard of since their flight from Mount Bay.

A few weeks later Beatrice there was an invite to the christening of her new nephew.

"I don't think I can travel that far these days," said her mother.

"I could go mother, I really would like to spend some time with my brothers and see all the children," said Beatrice. "There's a stage coach that goes down once a week I could catch that."

"Beatrice, if you are going to go then I want you to convince them to move away from the mines, maybe move to St Ives, lovely town so I'm told."

"Why don't you want them to stay in Mithraston?" Beatrice asked.

"Now that they have started families I want them out of that area."

"Presumably you are still worried about what the Garretts will try," said Beatrice.

"I keep my eyes and ears open and although they seem to have been thwarted when their plans for railways and canals fell through, I'm sure they are up to no good," concluded her mum.

"I'll see what I can do but with the collapse of the mining in the area no doubt they would be pleased to move on," said Beatrice. "So is there anything else I can do whilst I'm there."

"I haven't been able to contact Crystal recently, so if you could go the pool and see if she has any insights we need to know."

Beatrice started making plans for her trip and couldn't wait to find Luke waiting outside. She had already planned a new window and decided this would be the best way to entice him to come to the town.

"Very pretty as usual," whispered Luke's voice from behind her, as he admired the startling display she had made. A magical scene with plates depicting woodland glens as a backdrop to a 'stone circle' of small silver fairies dancing around central semi-precious agate stone with the look of a deep swirling pool.

"Thank you, I hoped you'd come over," said Beatrice. "I'm going on a trip to the west to see my family."

"Excellent that fits in with my planning," said Luke giving her a surreptitious hug. "Walk with me we don't want to be watched."

They walked slowly down the hill. "What's going on?"

"I thought this could be the ideal time to get married," said Luke.

"Really?" said Beatrice.

"Yes, we'll go on horse and get ahead of the stagecoach, get married, stay at the Coaching Inn and collect the stage the next day."

Beatrice didn't like hiding things from her mother but this was her future life after all. "I can't wait."

"I'll meet you at the stables of Wednesday morning."

"So why are you so excited?" asked Jeremy when she returned to the shop.

"I'm going to Cornwall to see the family," said Beatrice.

"Is that all?" asked Jeremy.

"Yes, what else could there be?"

"Nothing," said Jeremy with a knowing wink.

Are you going to be alright in the shop whilst I'm away?

"Of course," he said. "Your mother will help if necessary. You just go and enjoy yourself, and take care on the roads."

Beatrice awoke as sunshine peeped through a small gap in the curtains, wondering where she was. She had slept well after the dramatic events of the day; she exhilarating ride across the countryside; the quick wedding ceremony at a remote church and the wedding night joys.

She turned to Luke to snuggle up, to find an empty bed. "Luke, Luke, where are you? Don't hide now, don't be a tease." Silence surrounded her in the room.

She quickly washed in the bowl of cold water left in the room and dressed ready to try and find Luke no doubt setting up her wedding breakfast.

"Where's my husband?" she asked the inn keeper, when she found the dining room empty.

"He left very early," he said. "You'll have to be quick if you want to catch the coach it's ready to leave."

Hoping that Luke had gone ahead she grabbed her bags and hurried out. The horses breathe blowing steam trumpets in to the cool morning air; stamping their hooves, impatient to get off. The kindly driver took her luggage. "Do you want to go topside or inside?"

"On the top please, I want to see if my husband is ahead somewhere."

"Come up front then," he said taking her hand and helping her up.

Beatrice worried why Luke had left in such a hurry without telling her but was sure there would be a reasonable and hopefully an exciting reason.

Chapter 23 - Crystal Horrified

The stage arrived in the village and Beatrice had a sinking feeling, as Luke was nowhere to be seen. Her last hopes that he had gone ahead to prepare a family welcome, dashed.

She walked slowly to the family home full of fears that she had done something wrong on her wedding night and somehow annoyed Luke so much that he had just left. Arriving at the home she tried to put on a brave face as her relatives gathered around her all asking questions at the same time.

"Wait, wait, let her sit down," said Reginald. "She looks worn out."

"Not to say unhappy, what's the problem?" asked Demelza, Reginald's wife.

"Just very tired I'm sorry and that road was very dusty," said Beatrice wiping away some tears. She had no intention of burdening the family with her worries, at what should be a happy time for them. "Let me see the new baby."

Demelza handed over the chubby baby which Beatrice cradled in her arms. "He's lovely, hello Trevan."

"We named him after his grandfather," said a proud Reginald.

Sitting around the fire after supper, Beatrice had calmed down and sufficiently brightened up, "So where's Charlie?"

"I sent him off to Bristol to see if he can find new business premises," said Reginald.

"Mum will be pleased, she was hoping you'd move up to St Ives," said Beatrice.

"More of a den of smugglers up there, from what I've heard, not the big business that is in Bristol," said

Reginald. "Further away of course but it's the centre of trade."

"Not always a good trade I hear," said Beatrice, thinking of rumours of the slave traders up there.

"That's as maybe," said Reginald. "But there's more money to be had up there, compared to the dwindling mining in Cornwall,"

"Well at least you'll be away from here, Mum will be pleased with that, at least," said Beatrice. "And what of the Garretts?"

"As far as old man Garrett is concerned, we have heard that he has become a helpless gibbering idiot and has locked himself away in his big house," said Reginald.

"How did you hear that?"

"All secrets where there are servants, don't stay secret for long. Rumour has it that he thinks his place is haunted and keeps screaming out the names of his long-lost brothers, so I would think he is not long for this world."

"And his children?" Beatrice asked.

"Now that's another story" continued Reginald. "Nasty bunch of boys, certainly chips off the old block. They have become very influential around here by fair means or foul. We will definitely have to watch out for them."

"What have you heard?"

"Dodgy financial deals for starters, coupled with extortion, which seems to be in keeping with the family tradition! Their influence with local magistrates and police seems to keep them out of trouble," he continued. "The thing I can't understand though is that even when times are hard and their schemes fall through, they still seem to come out of it even richer."

Later when Beatrice and Demelza were alone, Demelza asked. "Tell me what's really wrong, Beatrice?"

"Is it that obvious."

"I'm afraid so."

"You won't tell the boys?"

"No, they know nothing of the affairs of the heart," said Demelza, kindly. "I assume it's a boy?"

"Well, supposedly my husband."

"Husband? I didn't know you were married."

"No-one knows. My mother wanted me to wait for a year but with this trip it seemed an obvious time to go through with the ceremony. But now I'm not so sure there was one, and now my 'husband' has disappeared."

"Oh dear, tell me everything and we'll see if we can make head or tail of it."

Beatrice told her the whole story from the moment Luke appeared at the shop, until she woke up this morning alone.

"We'll have to go to the church and look in their records; it's the only definitive way we could confirm what's going on."

"Are you sure? I hate to put you to so much trouble," said Beatrice.

"No trouble, we'll have this mystery cleared up in a trice," said Demelza. "Meanwhile a hot drink and a good night's sleep will do us good."

The next morning rode to the church where the ceremony had taken place, Beatrice continuing to look out for Luke in case he had been robbed and left for dead in some ditch.

They arrived at the country church to find the doors open and the priest kneeling at the altar, deep in prayer. After a few minutes of quiet contemplation, he stood and came over to them.

"Hello ladies, welcome to my church what can I do for you?" he asked. "Wedding bans; christening; or some prayers for loved ones?"

"No nothing like that, but we are curious about a wedding ceremony you performed on Tuesday," asked Demelza.

"Tuesday?" Queried the priest. "I was away in the north on Tuesday."

"So, who would have performed a wedding then?" asked Beatrice, with a sinking feeling.

"No-one that I know."

"But I signed the registry," said Beatrice.

"Let's have a look, shall we?"

They followed the priest into the vestry and he brought down the book, which Beatrice recognised as the one in which they had signed their names.

Opening it up the priest scored the names.

"It was on a new page," said Beatrice, "right at the top."

"Nothing I'm afraid."

"Look there," said Demelza. "Isn't that the remnants of a torn page."

"Indeed it is," said the priest. "Never mind, just bring your husband in and we'll sign it again, there's always a vandal or two in this parish I'm sure we can sort this out."

"We'll be in touch," said Demelza ushering Beatrice out before there were some awkward questions.

"There's definitely a problem here," said Demelza, "but I'm sure there's an explanation."

"I do hope so," said Beatrice, "but it does look as if I've been duped." And violated she thought.

Once home she told Demelza she would go off and consult with her old friends in the woods "Maybe they have some ideas."

She sat in the clearing in the woods by the magical pool, if indeed that's what it was, and through her tears tried to conjure up Crystal.

"Crystal please come and see me," she went through the ritual of petals and blood, but it was her great uncle and grandfather that appeared first.

'Hello, you must be Beatrice again,' said one.

'Grown a bit,' said the other.

'So how can we help?' said the first.

"Mother and I wanted to know how you have been getting on with Jan."

'Oh, what fun, what joy!' said one.

'Well not for Jan obviously!' said the other.

"I hear he is going mad, I assume that is your doing?"

'Oh yes, he sees monsters and ghouls everywhere! He can't go down into the cellar, without Methuselah waving her snakelike tentacles.' An image appeared in front of her of a head with snakes for hair.

"Scary," said Beatrice.

'And his study is full of growling monsters,' mouthed one. Another image appeared, apparently Jan's study, where growling green lion dogs were snarling and gnashing their teeth.

'And what about the octopus in his bed and the cockroaches crawling over him in his bed," said the other.

Images appeared of Jan's bedroom with Jan screaming at the sight of an octopus under his sheet and him writhing about slapping cockroaches that were crawling all over his body.

'And the toads in his boots and the worms in his food," added the first vision. Images appeared of squidgy toads jumping out of Jan's boots and a plate of food with squirming with worms.

Whilst thrilled at Jan's discomfort, which she felt was well deserved but it wasn't going to help her position.

"Thanks for showing me," said Beatrice, beginning to fell itchy herself. "But I really need to talk to Crystal."

'Oh, we were just beginning to have fun,' said the first.

'Yes, but Beatrice needs to talk to Crystal.'

'OK, OK, we'll go, Bye.'

'Bye.'

As they drifted into the darkness of the pool, in the sunlight, a small shimmering form appeared.

"Hello Beatrice," said the tiny sprite. "You've been away a long time, how are you?

"Not well, I'm afraid."

"You look in good health, which is fortuitous considering your condition."

"Condition?"

"Well the baby of course."

"Oh no, I can't be."

"Well you are," said the Sprite." But why are you carrying a Garrett baby?"

Chapter 24 – Cold Dishes

Beatrice crept through the back courtyard of their home and up to her mother's bedroom to find her sitting up in her bed. Beatrice held her finger to her lips so that her mother wouldn't shout out with pleasure.

"Hush mother," said Beatrice, giving her a heartfelt hug.

"Why do I have to hush."

"I need to talk to you in private before Jeremy gets back."

"Why, what's wrong?"

"Lots of things," said Beatrice.

"With the family?"

"No, me."

"Oh dear, is it something to do with Luke?" asked her mum.

"Yes."

"We told you nothing good would come of him."

"I know, I know, you told me to wait," said Beatrice. "But you know better than most what true love is."

"I've been lucky in love, I agree," said Brianna. "What did he do?"

"He was extremely clever," said Beatrice. "He set up a sham marriage, a vicar, documents and everything."

"That takes a lot of planning," said her mother.

"Let me show you the certificate I got, I needed it for the innkeeper." She pulled out the document and showed her mother.

"This looks genuine enough," said her mum. "What's the problem?"

"Firstly, his name is fake," continued Beatrice, "As is that of the 'vicar'. The page we signed in the registry has gone missing, as has Luke."

"Oh dear, but I assume there is something else?"

"Indeed, I spoke to Crystal at the pool and she told me I was carrying a Garrett baby."

"Garrett!" her mother exclaimed. "How could you?"

"SShhh, well I didn't know he was a Garrett," said Beatrice trying not to sob. "He told me his name was Luke Carr, which is what it says on the certificate."

"He has gone to elaborate lengths to get you into bed," said her mother. "Here come close, have a hug." As Beatrice's tears began to flow unchecked.

"What's going on," said Jeremy from the door. "I heard you cry out. Oh, you're back Beatrice. Welcome home."

"We're fine Jeremy," said Brianna. "I'll tell you all the news after breakfast. Now leave us for a bit please."

Mystified, Jeremy went back downstairs knowing arguing would do no good.

"What are you going to do?"

"I think I'm going to keep the baby, as for me it is still a love baby," said Beatrice wiping away her tears. "What I do about this Garrett boy is another matter."

"We can't let him get away with it, can we?" agreed Brianna.

"I have no intention of doing that," said Beatrice. "But I think first I need to confirm who he is and then work on from there."

"I'll tell Jeremy," said her Mum. "We'll talk again later,"

"I will I think I'll go and lie down for a bit, that journey from the mines is very tiring."

The next morning, she sat with her mother discussing some options.

"Have you got any ideas?" asked Brianna.

"I first need to determine if Luke really is a Garrett," said Beatrice.

"How are you going to do that? You're not thinking of going to their house?"

"No much too dangerous to confront him directly," agreed Beatrice. "But we know where they live, hopefully they try and pretend to be good citizens by going to local church."

"That would be the Methodist church."

"I believe there is a new one at St Erth," said Beatrice. "I'll try that first."

"Make sure you are disguised," said her mother. "You don't want 'Luke' to recognise you."

The next Sunday Beatrice waited outside the church in St Erth, to see if she recognised anyone, but despite a lot of locals gathering, none of the Garretts had appeared and certainly not her 'Luke'. She took her place in a quiet section of the upper gallery, observing the people below and around her. A small commotion from the entrance just as the vicar began the service and in trooped the Garrett family and took their pews at the front, two sons supporting the frail Jan.

"Luke!" said Beatrice, under her breath, "So Crystal was right."

"Sorry?" queried a young girl, dressed in a simple Sunday frock, sitting down next to her.

"Pardon, oh I was merely saying a prayer," said Beatrice. "I'm Crystal by the way." Beatrice had donned a simple dress which disguised her shape and a long scarf to hide her jet-black hair.

"Hello Crystal, I'm Tamsyn."

"Shush," said the matronly woman next to Tamsyn.

After the service including a long sermon on obedience and respect for one's betters, Beatrice followed Tamsyn the churchyard for some fresh air.

"Do you think the sermon was about us?" asked Tamsyn.

"Why?"

"All that stuff about obedience and respect," said Tamsyn. "I'm sure the Garretts put the vicar up to it."

"Do you know them?"

"The Garretts? Yes, I work in their house."

"Really," said Beatrice. "So is that why you think the sermon was arranged."

"Yes, they're not very nice people, but there's not much work around here," said Tamsyn. "Trumped up miners, lording it over their servants."

"You, you mean,"

"Yes, horrible people treat me like dirt and try to take advantage," said Tamsyn. "Then punish me for 'disobedience'."

"The father or the sons?" asked Beatrice.

"The son Duke, mostly," said Tamsyn. "But he'd better be careful, he's hoping to marry a local socialite."

"Really, who's that then?"

"Daughter of the local Stanneries Warden, Miss Seymore-Conway," she said. "Oh, time for me to go."

"Lovely to meet you Tamsyn," said Beatrice, as she saw the matronly woman approach.

"Will you be back?" asked Tamsyn.

"Oh yes we'll talk again soon," said Beatrice, drifting away.

"Did you find out anything?" asked her mother when she got home, dusty from the dry roads.

"More than I could have hoped for in one visit," said Beatrice, telling her mum about the talk she'd had with Tamsyn.

"Have you thought what you might do?" asked Brianna.

"I've got an idea to spoil his proposed marriage," said Beatrice.

"That's quick."

"It was a long ride home," said Beatrice. "Let me show you." Beatrice took the marriage certificate and flattened the creases on the bed.

""Look here," said Beatrice. "He's put his name as 'Luke Carr'. He obviously was worried about changing his name too much in case he was called out in the street."

"You say his real is Duke," said her mother. "You know I think I could change this to Duke Garrett quite easily."

"I thought you might see my plan," said Beatrice, knowing her mother's skills at calligraphy had been put to good use in the past.

"I'm not dead yet," she said. "Besides anything to get back at the Garretts will do me good. Fetch my quill and some black ink."

Beatrice went downstairs to fetch the writing equipment and returned upstairs.

"Open the curtains a bit more," said Brianna. "Pass me my board."

Beatrice watched as her mother practised the hand that had written the certificate. A hand that had painted thousands of china plates had not lost her touch.

"I think that's fine," said her mother. "Now give me the certificate."

Beatrice passed over the certificate as her mother carefully changed Luke Carr to Duke Garrett.

"Perfect," said her mother. "Now I think after that effort I need to sleep."

Beatrice kissed her forehead and closed the curtains. Waving the doctored certificate to dry the ink, she went back to her room and tucked it away safely.

"Hello Crystal," said a small voice beside her as she sat in the church a few weeks later

"Hello Tamsyn," replied Beatrice.

"I must see you outside afterwards," whispered Tamsyn.

The matronly woman gave a stern look at Tamsyn, so Beatrice squeezed Tamsyn's hand in reply, whilst pretending to concentrate on the service.

Once outside and in a quiet corner, Tamsyn burst out with "Guess what?

"What?" asked Beatrice.

"He's announced their engagement," said Tamsyn.

"What Luke?" said Beatrice. "I mean Duke."

"Yes, to the Wardens daughter," said Tamsyn. "They are so excited, finally climbing the social ladder."

"Why so quick," asked Beatrice.

"Can't you guess?" said Tamsyn, with a wink. "Up to his usual tricks no doubt."

Beatrice knew all about his tricks.

"I wish we could expose him, nasty boy," said Tamsyn.

"I do have a plan for that," said Beatrice. "I can't tell you in case you get questioned."

"I'm good at keeping secrets," said Tamsyn.

"Maybe so, but it's better for you not to know," said Beatrice. "However, I will need you to tell me if it works. When are you next here?"

"Every week."

"I'll see you in a couple of weeks, take care," said Beatrice.

"Bye Crystal."

Beatrice went back to church entrance to find the notice board and the notice of banns for Duke Garrett and Francis Seymour-Conway, which gave her the address she needed.

When she returned home she put the marriage certificate in an envelope addressed to the Lord Warden and, not trusting the new postal service, rode for two days to the ancestral home and personally delivered the document, hoping for the desired effect.

Two weeks later she went back to the church and immediately saw that the notice had been taken down. She had to wait patiently through the service before she could talk to Tamsyn.

They walked to a quiet corner under the Yew trees where Tamsyn couldn't contain her excitement, "You've done it."

"I don't know what you mean," said Beatrice, with a sly wink.

"Yes, you do, oh," said Tamsyn, catching on. "Of course not, I wonder what happened."

"So, the marriage is off then?" asked Beatrice, pretending ignorance.

"There's been an almighty row," said Tamsyn. "Apparently Duke's been accused of attempted bigamy."

"Gracious me! I wonder why that is?"

"So how did you pull that off, Crystal?" asked Tamsyn, not fooled by her innocent looks.

Beatrice decided to tell Tamsyn about the false marriage and the marriage certificate.

"Very clever. What a cad."

"Indeed. What has Jan done to Duke."

"He's confined him to the house for the foreseeable future," said Tamsyn.

"And Jan?"

"He's livid, and acting weirder than ever, hobbling around the house shouting about how he's been betrayed."

"He has been," said Beatrice.

"Yes, he was hoping to move up in the social world and all those hopes are dashed," said Tamsyn.

"Good, couldn't happen to a nastier man," said Beatrice. "Aren't his other sons good enough?"

"Those thugs?" said Tamsyn. "No, Duke was the only one to get a proper education, so all Jan's hopes were on him."

"What'll happen now do you think?"

"I heard him say that if he causes any more problems he'll ban him to the sugar plantations."

"Now there's a thought," said Beatrice.

"Do you have an idea?" asked Tamsyn.

"I have some thoughts but I may need your help this time," said Beatrice.

"Anything."

"Are you sure you're up for it, I wouldn't want you to lose your position."

"It's time for me to get a bit of revenge as well," said Tamsyn. "What do you need?"

"Well to start with I would want a sample of Duke's writing."

"That should be easy enough,"

"Meanwhile, I need to sort a few things out," said Beatrice.

Chapter 25 – Visions in a Pool

Beatrice watched vapours rise as the sun heated the dewdrops on the blades of grass. These long journeys to the wishing pool and to the Garretts home, would be the death of her, but she needed to talk to her ancestors to complete her plan.

Arriving at the pool and tying up her horse to the nearby tree, she sat down on one of the flat stones her mother had laid down many years ago. Collecting some of the perennial flowers and pricking her finger she invoked the spirits of the pool.

'Hello Beatrice," said the image of the fighting spirit, sparking in steam rising from the pool; sunlight flickering off her jewels and sword.

"Crystal how wonderful to see you," said Beatrice.

'How are you and how's your baby coming on?' said the apparition.

"We're both well," said Beatrice, rubbing her extending body. "Are Tom and Mark around?"

'Are you planning something for Jan?'

"Yes, and I need some help."

'Boys,' called Crystal.

Two gnarled faces appeared under the surface of the rippling water.

'Hello can we help?' they asked in unison.

Beatrice outlined her plans.

'You're as devious as us,' said Tom.

'We love it,' said Mark.

"Do you know where I can find what I need?"

'Yes, if you don't mind a bit of digging.'

"That's not a problem."

'You're not going to be squeamish?'

"It's just bones," said Beatrice.

The ghosts told her where she could find her surprise present for Duke. "Thanks for your help. Will you be there?"

'Wouldn't miss it. Good luck,' said Mark.

"Bye everyone."

Beatrice rode back across the moors on the way home, passing the area indicated by the ghosts. Getting on her hands and knees she started carefully separating the bracken and began digging through the loam to find the prize she desired, saddened by the ancient shallow grave. Arriving back at her home she wrapped the bundles up in tiny outfits she had made. She re-read the note she had crafted, copying the style of a letter by Duke that Tamsyn had given her.

'I know you love children so,

For what end I do not know,

These are beyond your reach,

Bled to death, by a leach'

Beatrice set out once more for the Garretts' Estate and a couple of hours later she arrived in the woods surrounding the home, waiting for Tamsyn to get away from the house. A twig cracked behind her and she spun around to be confronted by the game keeper, a huge double barrel shotgun pointing at her chest.

"What do we have here then," he said, making a lunge for her bundles.

"Get off, they're not game."

"We'll see about that," said the gamekeeper, grabbing Beatrice and pulling a bundle out of her hand.

Chapter 26 – Two in a Bed

"Fred stop that, it's just Crystal bringing me some clothes."

"Tamsyn, thank god for that," said Beatrice.

"It's alright Fred," said Tamsyn. "She's no poacher,".

"Oh, I didn't know she's a friend of yours," said Fred.

"I'll see you later," said Tamsyn. "We're just going for a long walk in the woods."

"He let me off easily," said Beatrice.

"He's sweet on my mother," said Tamsyn.

"Thank goodness," said Beatrice. "He could have undone all our plans,"

"What have you got there, Crystal," said Tamsyn.

Beatrice hated using the false name with Tamsyn but it was better she never knew who she really was. "They are two skeletons of babies abandoned centuries ago. I've wrapped them up in baby clothes to make them look real."

"What's the plan?"

"I am going to put them in Jan's bed once he's asleep," said Beatrice. "But I'll need your help to give me the all clear."

"He sleeps with his little helper, Laudanum, so once he's away he won't wake up, unless he has a really bad dream."

"Is that often?"

"Most nights, about 2 am, screaming about brothers and monsters."

"Well this will give him something real to scream about."

"Won't he suspect it was one of the staff?" asked Tamsyn. "There'll be hell to pay and me that gets it first."

"Not if he reads this note," said Beatrice, reading out the little poem she had written.

"Very clever," said Tamsyn. "So that's why you needed Dukes handwriting."

"Correct."

"Follow me and we'll get you hidden away in the attic where I sleep."

Tamsyn led Beatrice through the scullery door and up the back stairs up to the highest point in the house.

"You'll be safe here," she said. "No-one else comes up this far."

Beatrice made herself comfortable in a dark corner waiting for the night to fall, busying herself by making the skeletons as much like sleeping babies as possible, before dosing off.

"Crystal, Crystal, wake up," said Tamsyn softly.

"Is Jan asleep," asked Beatrice, rubbing the sleep from her eyes.

"Away with the fairies."

"Well, he'll soon have more than fairies on his mind," said Beatrice.

She followed Tamsyn back down the stairs to Jan's bedroom. They could hear the deep snores emanating from within the bedroom. Trying the door Tamsyn grimaced. "Locked!" she mouthed at her friend.

Beatrice dug into her pocket and withdrew her mother's master key and with a few adjustments soon had the door unlocked. Tamsyn slowly opened the door and peered through the gloom inside and was reassured by the site of Jan flat of his back, fast asleep. Beatrice, not wanting her friend to be caught ushered her out of the bedroom. She gently laid the baby skeletons against the footboard and lay the note between them.

She hid in the dressing room and wanting to witness the reaction. After an hour or so she decided that Jan wouldn't wake up without some help so she banged the door hoping. His body jumped and he snorted awake.

"What what's up!" he shouted, before seeing the two forms at the end of his bed and the note.

"Babies! Who put babies in my bed? Boys," he screamed as he backed up against the headboard, yanking at the bell pull. "Boys!"

Beatrice heard a commotion in the corridor and the sons burst into the room.

"What's wrong Dad?" shouted Gerald. "Another nightmare?"

They all watched in incredulity as the two skeleton babies awoke and wailed 'Mama! Papa!' and leapt into the air, flew across the bed and crashed down on Jan.

"Get them off. Get them off me," shouted Jan, flailing his arms as they repeatedly attacked him, before being knocked into the corners by Charles.

Jan continued to hit himself in uncontrollable spasms, and one of the sons held him down, whilst the other picked up the note. Duke stood by the door dumbfounded by the spectacle before him.

"What's the note say," asked Charles.

Gerald read Beatrice's poem out loud, adding. "This is your handwriting Duke."

"No nothing to do with me," said Duke.

"Oh, yes it is," said Gerald. "You know what Dad said. Now get to your room and pack."

No love lost there, thought Beatrice as she watched the scene unfold through the crack in the door. Beatrice decided she had heard enough and gently closed the door on the chaotic scene in the bedroom and upon turning was confronted by the ghostly forms of Mark and Tom.

'Did we do alright,' whispered Tom.

"What, oh yes wonderful," said Beatrice. "I thought it might be you."

'Least we could, do take care Beatrice.' as they faded into the wooden panels.

Beatrice quietly found her way out of the house and walked to her tethered horse in the woods before hearing a challenge from one of the windows.

"You!" called Duke. "This is all your doing."

"On the contrary," she replied. "You brought this on yourself, 'Luke' dear. Enjoy your exile."

Chapter 27 – Locked In

"I've heard from Tamsyn," said Beatrice, as she sat next to her mother's bed and held her weakening hand.

"Tamsyn?" queried her mother.

"My friend from the Garretts house," said Beatrice.

"Oh yes."

"She tells me that Jan had a massive apoplexy."

"I wish him dead for what he did to my sister and others no doubt."

"This is far worse; he still has his mind but is trapped in a body that won't function," said Beatrice.

"Hopefully he will have time to reflect on his dreadful deeds,"

Her mother drifted away.

"Mum are you alright?"

"Sorry darling but my time has come. You have done what I failed to do."

"Oh, I think you made him suffer as well."

"That's as maybe. But you keep clear of his sons."

"You have my word on that."

"And never let your guard down, they will not forgive or forget."

"I've suffered at their hands and won't let them get away with anything."

"Good, now remember I'll always be with you and inside of you whenever you need me," said Brianna, as she quietly drifted away.

Beatrice held her still hand, never again to make wonderful objects. Her tears dripped onto her mother's lifeless body and she remembered all the trials of her life, fighting her wicked uncle, but then reflected on the triumphs of her creative spirit.

The End

Printed in Great Britain
by Amazon